10p

AN ANGEL IN WAITING

Also by Jane Bailey

Promising

AN ANGEL IN WAITING

Jane Bailey

First published in 1997
by HEADLINE BOOK PUBLISHING

A HEADLINE REVIEW hardback

10 9 8 7 6 5 4 3 2 1

British Library Cataloguing in Publication Data

Bailey, Jane
An angel in waiting
1.English fiction – 20th century
I.Title
823.9'14[F]

ISBN 0 7472 1687 8

Typeset at The Spartan Press Ltd
Lymington, Hampshire

Printed in England by
Clays Ltd, St Ives plc.

HEADLINE BOOK PUBLISHING
A division of Hodder Headline PLC
338 Euston Road
London NW1 3BH

To Frank and Shirley

Magnolia

Keith Pooley opened the door, plunger in hand, and saw a youth with a dark ponytail and a questioning smile.

'Yes?' said Keith Pooley.

A pause. A swallow. 'Dad?'

A very long pause. Keith's hand went up to his own dark curls and smoothed them back, then seemed unable to let go. 'Carol?'

'Er – I'm a bloke. Gabriel.' Embarrassed laugh. 'This *is* 23 Church Road? Mr Morrison?'

'Ah, no!' Sweating, hot and cold. 'This is Church *Terraces*. Church Road's up there. You want the house that's being done up – couple of hundred yards on the right, look.'

'Cheers!'

He watched foolishly as the youth slung a canvas bag on his shoulder and walked towards a momentous meeting. Keith had waited for such a reunion with his daughter for eleven years, and for a moment he'd wondered – against all the evidence – if this lad could have been her. His pulse returned slowly to normal as he went back to unblock the sink in the kitchen, and to the minor chores that would help fill the rest of his day off.

Keith Pooley was born to the sound of 'Peggy Sue' on the wireless in a council house in Moorhampton. On his eighth birthday he had played Blind Man's Buff and danced to a new hit single, 'Money Can't Buy Me Love', and believed it. When he went to secondary school he believed it and when he met Linda Tilley he still believed it. Linda had been way out of his league, they said. A peach of a girl with a wide face and a mouth that stretched from ear to ear. She wore hipsters and looked good in them, and miniskirts with suede knee boots that seemed to melt into the curves of her calves. She didn't bother with the boys at school. She dated men with real jobs from Tibbles' Plastics and Sharpe & Fisher. Keith Pooley was way out of the running with his apologetic satchel and felt blazer with the arms too short because there was no point buying a new one for the last year of school. They reckoned Linda only took an interest in him when his dad got to be a bit famous, becoming West of England bowls champion and winning a trip to Florida. Also he knew a relative of George Best (or so they said). At any rate, Linda started sitting next to him in class and allowing her Deep Purple graffitied schoolbag to be carried. When he left school at sixteen and got a job at Tibbles' Plastics she was already flirting with his quality control inspector. But when he bought a motorbike at eighteen and asked her to marry him she swung her long curtains of centre-parted hair, stroked her choker, and said, 'Yes.'

They were married in a register office, Linda in a bright pink midi-dress with matching platform clogs, and he in dark grey flannel with a plain white shirt. That shirt was the beginning of the end, perhaps, he sometimes recalled. She had wanted a pink shirt (much the rage at the time) but he had gone for white. He guessed that was him: just a plain, uncolourful sort of man. No limelight, please.

Cameron Morrison stirred his emulsion paint with the end of a wooden spoon. He was a happy man. He had a pot of tea brewing in the kitchen and eight weeks of creativity ahead of him. 'Lovely day!' shouted Mrs Ferabee, catching sight of her new neighbour from her vantage point in the apple tree.

'Yes, isn't it?' said Cameron, looking round, a little startled, and seeing a woman with tight curly hair who could have been thirty or fifty. Then, because he thought something else was probably required of him, he said, 'I'm Cameron Morrison. We're your new neighbours. I'm trying to do this place up.'

'You've got your work cut out for you there, then.'

Cameron cast a proprietorial glance over the detached ramshackle building he had bought for his family. He had replaced the rotting window frames here at the back, lifted various floorboards in the living room ready for rewiring, exposed the damp behind the plaster in some of the rooms, and now he was painting some rendering on the extension. Rhona would have a bedroom large enough to invite her friends back to and wouldn't have to share when her gran came to stay. And there was a tin-roofed concrete building attached to the house at the back which he would turn into a granny annexe, so that his mother would not have to spend all her time in the nursing home. Of course, it wouldn't be finished overnight, but he had eight weeks, and in those eight weeks he was going to transform this shell into a mansion. Tina would love him for it. He had promised this for years now, and he knew she had suspended belief for long enough. Even by the time his wife brought Rhona home this afternoon she would see a change in the newly fitted windows gleaming with paint. He smiled as he thought how she would come and kiss him on the neck, nuzzle into him and tick him off for not protecting his hair from specks of white gloss.

Where Church Terraces merged into Church Road a small frizzy-haired girl was standing on the pavement outside Moorhampton primary school. Rhona was amazed to see her grandmother still sitting in the back of the car when her step-mother picked her up from school. She plonked her little plastic tuck box in the glove compartment. 'What do they mean, look after her *for the time being*?'

Tina sighed and started the engine. 'They assessed her, and they say the illness isn't advanced enough for her to be taken into care yet.' She looked in her rear-view mirror as if redirecting her comments. 'She can be better cared for in the community, it seems.'

'But she's off her trolley!' Rhona turned round and eyed her grandmother. Bubbles sat serenely, smiling back at Rhona as if she'd been paid a compliment. Her blonde perm sat on her head like a vanilla ice-cream scoop and her large breasts flopped over two mismatching belts.

'I think Japan's a good place for me to go. I haven't been to Japan.'

'Yes, why don't you go to Japan!' said Rhona, and turning back to her mother she said, 'See?'

Tina did her best to calm her daughter while negotiating the school traffic and her own feelings of despondency. She wasn't sure how Cameron would take it either. Still, it *was* his mother, and he might at least have some sense of guilt or duty to soften the blow. *She* was the one who would be doing the caring. Suddenly their dream cottage transformed itself. Instead of roses round the door and afternoons in deckchairs, she pictured Bubbles escaping down drainpipes and rescue parties searching for her in neighbourhood gardens and pubs. Perhaps Cameron would be able to afford to pay for private nursing with his new job. In a few years.

'Do they have proper toilets?' asked Bubbles, suddenly perturbed.

'Who?'

'In Japan.'

'You're not going to Japan,' sighed Rhona. 'More's the pity.' She was momentarily distracted by the back of a beautifully ponytailed young man walking on the far side of the road, who reminded her of her favourite pop star.

'How was school?' asked Tina brightly.

Rhona stopped craning her neck, scrunched her mouth to one side and said nothing.

'Did you make any nice friends today?' Tina wished she hadn't said 'nice'; it was too patronising for a nearly-eleven-year-old. And surely all friends were nice, weren't they? The trouble was, Rhona didn't have any. Tina knew her stepdaughter missed her friend Lucy who had moved away last year. Rhona was the sort of girl who made friends slowly. With her bony frame and thick glasses she did not immediately attract other girls. She would probably undergo weeks or months of name-calling before she was accepted by some group or other. Her pale flossy hair stood out like the kind of bristle dish brush given away free with saucepan sets at market stalls. She was the kind of girl who said nothing in crowds but in intimate company was hard to shut up. Her clear blue eyes would take everything in, and she would observe from behind her spectacles the slightest change of expression in the girls who sat in front of her in class and the tiniest hairs on their necks. She wore home-made clothes because, to

Tina's mind, clothes from fashion shops didn't last two minutes. Home-made clothes could last a lifetime. *That*, Rhona would say, was the problem.

Rhona still hadn't answered. She scratched at the pop stickers on her tuck box (Wig from the group When) and examined old car park tickets in the glove compartment.

'Mum, *promise* me she'll never come and meet me from school.'

Next door to the Morrisons' new home, the Ferabees' was the last in a short line of terraced council houses marking the end of the countryside and the outskirts of the town. They had bought theirs in the eighties, and it was the only council house in the row roofed with Provençal tiles and sporting a scrolled ironwork balcony and a conservatory. Across a back lawn dotted with concrete statuettes from Texas Homecare, Mrs Ferabee perched on a ladder in her apple tree awaiting more conversation. After a pause which became uncomfortable she turned and retied a yellow washing line around the fattest branch.

She heard Cameron say, 'Can I help you?' She smiled and looked across at her neighbour, but he wasn't addressing her. He was looking at someone by the side of his house, obscured by the fence. 'That's me,' she heard him say. She could make out a male voice but not what was said. And this was a pity, because the effect of it on her neighbour was clearly startling. He had had his back to her, a couple of steps up the ladder, but as he turned towards the speaker she saw a look of disbelief spread over his face. In shock, it seemed, he sat down heavily on the end of a trestle and a kettle of emulsion paint catapulted into the air, landing upside down on his head.

Heavy dollops of Magnolia paint ran down his chest and covered his struggling hands. He was ruining a good T-shirt, she found herself thinking in her panic. For a second she thought he looked like a circus clown, and maybe this was his idea of a practical joke. In a moment the other man would appear with a red nose, colossal feet and a custard pie. A lion would jump through a hoop and everyone would cheer. But a young man appeared and hovered for a moment, dancing this way and that to avoid the paint, unsure how to approach the swirling tin-headed man. Then her new neighbour collapsed to the ground, and the oily, cream-coloured fingers pounding the tin fell limp. The stranger crouched over him, struggling to remove the pot.

'*Help!*' he screamed. 'Someone, *help me*!'

'I'm coming!' shouted Mrs Ferabee to the young man's back. 'I used to be a nurse! You get an ambulance!'

He darted off in the direction of the road and she clambered down her stepladder. The taut yellow clothes line sank to the ground and flags of washing floated a retreat from the tree to lie limp on the crazy paving. She scurried round to the next door garden to try and help. It seemed far too pleasant a day for a fatality. But the paint kettle was stuck fast, and there was no sign of a pulse. She heard a car in the driveway and the engine putter to a stop. A car door slammed and then another. Mrs Ferabee would have to introduce herself to her neighbour by telling her that her husband had suffocated in a can of quick-drying emulsion.

Forget-Me-Not

Tina had been a plump, passive baby with soft springs of brown hair. She was carted about by her elder sisters: wheeled in toy prams, plopped into boxes, and yanked from one place to another in ungainly clutches. She was the fifth of five children. Her successes and failures were less significant than theirs; she was a post-afterthought, and grew up without anyone noticing.

They had all moved to different towns or counties before she left school. Even her father lived away in the Forest now with her eldest sister, and she hadn't seen him for a while. Her mother was a memory: a soft mound of flesh that cushioned them against the world. There were other things – white goose-pimpled ankles and a certain cotton dress that always smelt of detergent – but it was her softness that Tina chose to remember. Her father had mended TVs. He was a strict man who always had the last word, but he would sit by the fire with children climbing over him like kittens. They pulled his hair and emptied his pockets, while he tapped his pipe on the grate.

At school she became knock-kneed and smiled at jokes she didn't understand. Later, she grew to look much like her friends and smiled in lessons she didn't understand. She had two ambitions: to become a fashion designer, and to marry and start a family. The two things were envisaged entirely separately, so that they never seemed to clash with one another.

It came as a shock at sixteen to be pregnant and to have to make choices. She chose to keep the baby, whereas her boyfriend, Dermot, did not think it such a good idea. He howled and ranted and swore he would never marry her. Then he softened, and promised to marry her in a few years' time if she got things sorted. Wouldn't it be better, after all, to finish his craft apprenticeship in car mechanics and find a job first? Then they could be married properly and have babies galore. He even gave her a clannad ring to be going on with. Tina said, 'Oh well, then,' and spent all night sweating and torn. In the morning she decided: she did not want to spend the rest of her life saving 'ten pence off' vouchers and wearing acrylic.

Dermot was pleased, but then (remembering that he was a Catholic) added that it was a mortal sin and he would burn in hell fire if he were to agree to it. But as it was her decision, it was OK. Better for him just to keep out of it. She looked troubled then, and worried about what would happen to the baby. She wanted *this* baby, this baby again in a few years' time, and could he promise her absolutely it would be all right? He said it would just slip up to heaven to be an angel for a bit; then when they were ready, it would come down again and they'd all be happy. Tina said, 'Oh well, then, if you're sure,' and gazed in a watery way at her tummy.

She was told to count from one to ten, and that was the last she saw of the doctor. Outside the clinic a man in an anorak waved his arms at her and called her a murderer, and she was spat at by a woman in a bobble hat. Dermot told her not to worry and bought her a keyring with a plastic puppy on it. Two years later he got a job fixed up and went round the world on a motorbike with a girl called Holly or Polly or Poppy or something, who kept ponies.

After Cameron's death Mrs Ferabee took care of Rhona and Bubbles for the day. Tina wandered from room to room trying to establish some kind of order in her head. It still felt like a practical joke. Any moment now Cameron would reappear. His boots by the back door still had fresh grass on them and socks stuffed in them which still smelt of him. One paintbrush still stood in a jar of Polyclens on the draining board and fingerprints of pale paint gave him away. The bathroom sink had black bits from his shaver, and the soap in the bath had a lone pubic hair attached to it. In the bedroom a little pool of clothes lay by the bed where he had dropped them; his trouser pocket had this week's lottery number in it (she prayed it wouldn't win), and the sheets were still crumpled in exactly the position he had left them. Back in the kitchen a pot of tea had brewed and stewed on the window sill, and a biscuit had a mouth-sized piece taken out of it: his mouth. An airmail writing pad on the table was evidence of the letter he had written to his brother in Australia, no doubt informing him of his new job, the bargain purchase, his mother's illness being taken care of in a home and everything coming up roses. Even now that letter was wending its way across the globe, thought Tina, and Cameron's brother would read a letter from a dead man.

It seemed impossible that the house could have once been their dream home in embryo. Now it seemed a carcass. Its raised floorboards leaning neatly against the living room wall seemed to mock her. Its stained plaster and patches of bare brickwork were saying, 'Tough shit!' The whole house with its grand unfurnished plans and unopened paint pots was a cruel joke.

Tina wore the same clothes as one day followed the next, forgot to wash her hair or look in mirrors. She dreaded meeting people, in case she had to talk about Cameron, and found herself avoiding the few friends she had. The house was a picture of gathering chaos. New floorboards were stacked in the hall with rolls of discount carpet, and vanloads of cement, sand and plaster were still arriving and dumping themselves in the living room or along the staircase. There were tea chests everywhere, and upstairs there were pools of clothes and unemptied cardboard boxes in every room. These lay in wait, emotional booby traps waiting to ambush her. She let them lie.

Tina told people he had fallen off a ladder to avoid the constant retelling of the undignified event; she couldn't bear anyone to think it funny. Was his death more tragic because of the farcical circumstances? Tina couldn't say. But something made Cameron's exit from the world at this precise moment worse than any ordinary death, she felt. It wasn't just his absence or his suffering. It was as though he had deliberately played a trick on her.

Cameron had been born into one of those well-to-do families

whose sons drop out of university to find themselves. Cameron had still been looking at twenty-eight, when he married Lisa and found a job as a building labourer. He felt he had it all at last until Lisa gave birth to Rhona and was promptly run over outside the mother and baby clinic five weeks later. Tina found him a couple of years on, a doe-eyed widower not coping with baby rusks and potty training. She was no genius, Tina, she knew that. People found her self-effacing and malleable. But Cameron, when he ordered his chocolate milkshake, had found her shrewd, street-wise and inquisitive. He liked what he called her 'not ready' look, a heap of long brown curls always stuffed into something shaggy: a creased scarf or a raggedy ribbon. Not long after their marriage he decided to go back to college to study law. He had watched his father squander the family fortune on gambling and die an alcoholic. He was going to bring home real money and see to it that his own family wanted for nothing. When he qualified they would live in a rose-covered cottage and Tina could stay at home, have babies and suchlike. Meanwhile she had supported him for years with her waitressing job at the Happy Sausage, ticking her fertile days on the baked bean calendar by the till, ready for 'D-Day'.

And here it was at last. Just last month they had sold their terraced house which opened on to a pavement, a bus stop and dog excrement. He had transferred their negative equity to the purchase of this wreck of a house at the same price they had sold. But – and this was the point – a wreck with *potential*. He had eight weeks before his new job as a solicitor commenced, and by then the house would be worth twice what they paid for it.

But all that had disappeared with the letter she had just received. Cameron's employer (P. J. Coney, Solicitor), although not a man she could even remember meeting, had written a touching tribute to her husband along with the information that she had been left with massive negative equity, no will and no life insurance. There would probably be some state benefits she was entitled to. He offered his advice free of charge. Tina reread the letter slowly and put it back in its envelope. The house was worthless as it was, and she couldn't afford to have it renovated by outsiders. She had left her job at the Happy Sausage when they moved and now she would have to find another. There would be no babies, no jam-making, no Cameron. He had wiped her out. He hadn't even left her to start her life from scratch; he had left her with huge debts, his orphan daughter and his batty mother.

Each of her sisters rang in turn to commiserate. 'Time is a great healer,' said Ellen, helpfully, and, 'At least you've got the house,' from Katrina (who hadn't seen it). Julie said, 'Babies aren't everything, you know, Teen. You don't wanna go having babies. You'll be up all night, changing nappies, wiping puke, it's not everyone can cope. And *then* they grows up and don't wanna know you. Bloody well out of it if you ask me!' Patsy took a different tack. 'I know *loads* of women who have children late in life. You've bags of time!' She cited the exception as if it were the rule – that always did the trick, she found: 'Our Eileen's friend had one at forty-four! See? How old are you now? Thirty-six? Well there you go – you could fit five in!'

But Tina knew about broken nights. She pottered around every evening finding things to do. Bed seemed like defeat: having to give in to loneliness and lie in the dark listening to the silence and the first whir of the milk float at four. She knew about puke too. Hadn't she brought Rhona up and mopped up her spilt juice and far-flung baked beans? Hadn't she potty-trained, nappy-changed, nursery-rhymed and kissed-it-better for the last nine years? And if that wasn't enough, all her sisters knew she'd had some other experience which was never spoken of.

She looked out of the kitchen window and stared at the scene of the accident, horrified that she should be wondering at that moment whether the huge paint marks could be removed from the patio slabs. She let her head drop back over the chair and tried to think. She spotted an old paint-covered overall on the back of the chair and sank her nose into it. It was a long time before the light seeped out of the room and the others returned. Then she padded up the stairs in his overall, her hands completely covered by the long empty arms.

The funeral was a scorching Friday at the beginning of May. Rhona had cried a little in private, but appeared quirky and quiet in front of others. Only two weeks before she had known an intense grief when her favourite pop star, Wig, had been reported missing on the News at Ten. He had disappeared, and there were worries for his safety. Rhona had wept inconsolably and walked around in a daze, her vision blurred by tears. Every pop singer she saw reminded her of him, and she locked herself away to listen to his latest hit single over and over again, reading tragic messages into the lyrics. Everything she saw was a sign from Wig (a run-over cat, thunder and lightning, a bald man in the Co-op). Her panic for the safety of this man whom she had never met seemed odd now compared to her plugged-up emotions over her father. She had an awkward feeling that something more public and hysterical was expected of her, and she was vaguely aware that there was a point somewhere she hadn't quite reached. She felt she was camping out and couldn't find a thing to wear in her suitcase or in the wardrobe which had been moved to the centre of the room away from the wall. It was the time of year when insects appeared from nowhere: spiders, moths, flies, and all manner of creatures with an unacceptable number of legs. She wasn't happy with her new surroundings, and the unsettled feeling seemed to give her grief a temporary, unfixed quality. She wanted something solid to cling on to. Only then would she really be able to let go.

The service was a sad, frugal affair, paid for by Tina's family who were not well off themselves. Tina couldn't help thinking, as he slid behind the crematorium curtains, that Cameron would have protested at the tacky joints in the coffin timber. Cameron's brother couldn't get a flight out in time and so the gathering consisted only of her father and one sister, Bubbles, Mrs Ferabee, Rhona and herself, along with one of Cameron's student friends and a trainee solicitor or two. Mrs Ferabee had kindly invited them all back to her house for sandwiches, for which Tina was endlessly grateful. As yet she knew no other neighbours and a wake in their house – Cameron's work in progress – would have been too depressing. And no venue would have been ideal for this peculiar mixture of guests. Bubbles had cried and raged sporadically for three days and nights, but had nodded off during the funeral service and now seemed perversely chirpy. The student cracked awkward jokes about Cameron's bad timing, and one of the trainee solicitors developed a sudden unaccountable interest in the cheap ornaments and wedding photographs which lined the mantelpiece. Eight years ago she felt sure Cameron's parents had quietly disapproved of her family and her strong local accent. She remembered this now as she watched her father and eldest sister nod with interest as Bubbles told them she didn't think much of the best man.

Rhona felt panicked by the assembly of odd people. She slipped out to the hallway and trotted a small china horse across the hall table. She became aware of someone watching her, and looking up she saw Joel, the Ferabees' nine-year-old son, lolling over the banister. As she looked up he ducked slightly and only his dark head, resting on his arms, appeared over the wooden slats. She had met him before and ignored him. He went to the same primary school and had hovered around like an imbecile when the Ferabees had looked after her some days ago. Now they exchanged stares.

'What are you staring at?' she said, putting down the horse but feeling that age was on her side.

'Nothing,' he said after a while, retreating still further. He felt awed by this girl whose father had died. He hardly dared speak to her in case she burst into tears.

'Do you want to play a game?' he asked at last.

'Not really,' she said, remembering to look tragic.

This seemed to get them nowhere.

'What sort of a game?'

'Anything.'

'Well, what've you got?'

'Face paint . . .' he trailed off as if there were a list, but got stuck.

Rhona sighed, unaware of the irony of this suggestion. She was too old for face paint, but preferred this company to that in the living room.

'Have you got any make-up?'

'I can get you some.'

They disappeared into his bedroom, and the discovery that he had a collection of music by her idol, the singer Wig from the group When, brought her round to play with him the following day as well.

The day after the funeral, a Saturday, Tina toured the house with a notepad and pen, inspecting all its gaping wounds. Her aim was to make at least one room habitable for the time being, while she worked out how to tackle the mortgage. Armed with a list of necessities, she took the car to the nearest DIY store.

The Morrisons' house must have been a picture once. Its pale stone walls were surrounded by gardens – laid to lawn to the front and rear and once dug for vegetables on its west side. It was in Moorhampton on Church Road, a pretty country road with its own village church and primary school, but which grew into a thick noisy highway as it spidered into the centre of the nearby town. To the west of the house the road petered into stone cottages with the occasional thatch, worthy of magazine covers. To the east was the row of council houses, the primary school, a post office and a couple of shops. This was the direction Tina took, and she followed the road for a mile until it widened and the houses thinned to make way for garages, garden centres and trading estates. She pulled up in the car park of Did-It-Myself, the largest DIY store this side of town.

She trailed along aisles of timber, front doors, back doors, window frames and woodseal. This was Cameron's territory, she thought. On cold winter Sundays he had basked in the Did-It-Myself aisles for hours, while she fended off the double glazing salesman at the exit and Rhona, in her younger days, bobbed endlessly back and forth in the slot machine aeroplane in the foyer.

She looked at the first item on her list: 'Stuff for rot – wood, bricks, plaster'. Since there wasn't an aisle called Rot she decided to seek advice. She saw a portly young man in a blue overall counting toilet seats, and asked if he had any product to get rid of rot. He stood up and looked at her, chewing.

'What sort of rot?' he asked, examining her jeans and pullover with a sweep of his eyes.

'Well, floor and wall. The wood is rotten. And then on the walls the plaster's rotten, and behind that . . . I think the stone's OK . . .'

'Dry rot, then?'

'I expect so.'

'You wanna get someone in to take a look at that, love. You won't be able to do that yourself, look.'

She noticed his fashionable haircut and morning-after stubble. He had probably been out on the town the night before, she thought, surprised for a moment that life went on as usual for other people.

'Thanks, but I can't afford to pay anyone.'

'Look, love, *you* won't get that tackled on your own.'

'I'd rather do it myself,' she said limply. 'What do I need?'

He put his tongue in his cheek and scratched his nose. 'Right.' Then he looked her up and down and chewed his gum some more. 'Floor: most likely cause is your faulty dpc allowing moisture to pass to your inner leaf of the wall at skirting board level . . .'

'Dpc?'

'Damp proof course to you, love. If it's your dpc you can pressure-impregnate your wall with damp resisting fluid – aisle twelve. Crumbling plaster: cut it out with a bolster chisel – you've got one of those, I expect, haven't you, love? Club-hammer it back to your brick. Then you want some Polyplasta – aisle two. Take it just proud of your surrounding area and rub it back down. But if you've got *dry* rot none of that'll be any good, look.'

He patted his top pocket as though looking for something. Tina noticed a small eggy stain on it, with 'Did-It-Myself' embroidered in red underneath. He drew out a sheaf of yellow cards.

'ACE Damp Busters,' he said, handing her one. 'My brother-in-law, but I can recommend him. There's a lot of sharks out there . . .'

'All right, Gary?' came a voice from a dark blue figure to the side. Gary's toilet lid fell open with a bang. He put the cards away and took the pencil from behind his ear.

'Can I be of assistance, madam?'

Tina looked at a man as tall as the wood-stained front doors and remarkably narrow for his height. They clearly didn't make uniforms to suit his awkward shape. A label attached to his too short, too ample jacket read: 'Keith Pooley'.

'I'm not sure if I have dry rot or wet rot and I'd like to tackle it myself. I can't afford damp people.'

Keith looked immediately sympathetic. 'Well, they're all worse than useless, anyway. Is there any red dust present?'

'No.'

'And fungus?'

'No.'

'Well, I doubt it's dry rot. And the wood – cracks along the grain or across *and* along?'

'I'm not sure – some's been replaced, I think.'

Gary was busy stocktaking again, hunched contritely over his toilet seats. The tall man put a bony hand on his chin and led her down the aisle. 'I can suggest something to start you off, I think.'

He walked down the aisle, moving in waves with the graceful gait of a giraffe.

'Do you live far?'

'Moorhampton.'

'Oh well! So do I! I'll tell you what, I can pop over and take a look if you like, on my way home. Then I'll get you sorted out with the equipment you'll need.'

Tina would normally have declined, but she wasn't in a position to be choosy. She was toying with the idea of consulting dozens of DIY manuals instead, when it struck her that this man's gawky, earnest face had a reliable quality to it.

'Thanks very much. That's really kind of you. Church Road, number twenty-three – just past the council houses and before the church.'

'Ah!' He was intrigued, but nodded and said nothing more. Then she enquired about a cashier's job she'd seen advertised at the entrance.

Rhona and Joel were exploring in what would have been her father's tool shed, having caked themselves in Mrs Ferabee's cucumber face pack. Rhona had tied two plastic flower pots together and was attaching them to her chest.

'We're on a desert island,' said Joel, tugging at a mud-covered tarpaulin in the corner. 'We need to make a den.'

He set about gathering pieces of plywood and rusty long-handled garden tools, chatting all the while about the plot of their adventure. Suddenly, he stood very still and stopped talking.

'There!' said Rhona, sporting a pair of blunt-ended breasts at last. 'What do you think?'

Joel still didn't speak. He looked at her and swallowed a couple of times.

'Good, isn't it?'

His mouth seemed stuck in a half-open position.

'What is it?' she asked.

He signalled to the corner of the shed where, protruding from the tarpaulin, was a human hand.

Wheatgerm

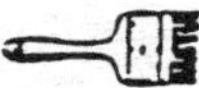

The house was south-facing, an old Cotswold stone construction with a rendered extension that must once have been painted white. At the rear, a tumbledown annexe – also rendered – jutted out on the ground floor with a part slate, part corrugated tin roof. There was a small cellar beneath the dining room, entered by a door in the hallway. To the left, the west half of the house – with living and dining rooms – was wooden-floored, whereas the right half of the house – which housed the kitchen in the front – had solid floors. Outside a gabled porch marked the centre of the building and the front door.

The kitchen was entered by a side door with its own white wooden porch, and opened on to a short path which curved through a vegetable patch to join the main front path on the east side of the building. Here, a rough rubble drive had been created, just wide enough for a car to park in, reaching almost to the house which was set some forty feet back from the road. It was surrounded by garden but, to the west, gardens stretched for over a hundred yards, bordered by the hedges of cow fields.

The house had a colourless, unloved look to it. The window frames had all been replaced but were mostly unpainted, and the panes looked blank and lifeless. The guttering was broken and tiles were missing from the roof.

Keith Pooley spent over an hour examining the place. He wandered from room to room collecting evidence – flaking pieces of wood and plaster in his hands, visiting the bathroom to check for any spores, emerging with new questions about the cistern and airing cupboard, and standing to stare for an unreasonable amount of time at portions of wall, scratching his chin slowly. Tina felt guilty for wishing he would be less meticulous. She regretted offering him a cup of tea.

'What you need is a better pourer,' he said, inspecting the teapot spout. 'This one may look nice, but he won't pour you a good cup. You want to go to Mace's on the High Street – they've got seconds there as good as new. A good plain pot, that's what you need. Now, he's a nice-looking pot, I'll grant you,' he pointed at Tina's white and blue china teapot as if it were in a Mr Universe line-up, 'but he's not going to pour you a good neat cup. Spout's all up the creek, see?' He indicated the fancy curves as if plainness were a virtue, and added quickly, 'Don't get me wrong. I like beauty along with the next man, but this here's not what you might call practical.'

Tina watched his practical hands, the spatulate fingers nervously turning a teaspoon from end to end on the tablecloth.

'Well, I'd better show you what tools I've got already,' she said, standing up when the last inch of tea in his cup showed no signs of going down.

'Right . . .'

He was interrupted by a scream from the garden.

Tina jumped nervously. 'Whatever was that?'

Keith glided to the window and peered out, his chiselled head perched on the long neck. 'Ha! They look a sight – enjoying themselves, though. They yours?'

Tina nodded. 'Well, one of them, sort of.' What was Rhona up to, enjoying herself? Her father was dead not twelve days and she was running around squealing.

Keith couldn't shift the picture of recent events out of his head. He knew from gossip that Mr Morrison had died, and since he had entered the house he had felt uneasy. The blue flashing lights of the ambulance outside it just a few days earlier kept flickering again in his mind, and all just moments after that earnest young man had left him. He wondered nervously if he perhaps held a secret, if he knew some evidence that might be relevant to the death of her husband. 'You don't have a son, then?'

'No.'

Or perhaps two secrets.

'Just Rhona,' she added in a tremendous hurry.

'I had a little girl,' he said, returning to the teaspoon.

'Oh, I'm sorry,' said Tina, suddenly aware, a little late, of the impact of 'had'. 'I'm so sorry.'

'Oh, no, she's not dead. Good as, though. Wife left and took her to America. No idea where. Never even sent me a photo. She must be thirteen by now, but she's still two to me. That's the last time I saw her.' He traced a rosebud in the tablecloth pattern with his finger. Then he placed the teaspoon down on the table and rose quickly.

He chatted about costings and followed her to a tea chest in the hall, crammed with oily canvas bags and boxes. From where she stood Tina could see the view from the hall window: a prettily shaped oak tree and a green patchworked hill behind. This is where she had had her last real conversation with Cameron. 'Now we can start a family,' he had said. 'You see, I'm a man of my word. Whenever you're ready, Tina, we can try for a child.' They had looked out at that tree, its pale new leaves gleaming in the mellow evening light, and she had felt rooted for the first time. She could grow and spread out at last. He kissed her, right there by the hat stand. He was keeping an eight-year-long promise, or so he thought, but in the end he broke even that unwittingly.

She pulled out a power drill, and something in the faraway look in her eyes must have struck her visitor, for he stopped his banter and looked at her intently: a sad, understanding look. Then he crouched on the floor to rummage through the bags, and his bent knees seemed skeletal under his trousers, so that had they been hinged the other way, he would have looked like an enormous stork.

'Do you have any references?' he said at last.

'References?'

'For the job. You're still interested, aren't you? I don't reckon there'll be a problem. Can you come in tomorrow?'

'Of course.'

'I'll get a list drawn up of what you'll need and I'll do a costing for you. But I'll tell you what, Mrs Morrison—'

'What?'

He frowned apologetically, 'I think you're going to have a job to do all that work yourself.'

'I expect I am.'

'I'm not doubting your ability – or whoever's doing it for you – but, well, if you need a hand or anything . . .'

It occurred to Tina that she had always needed a hand where practical matters were concerned, dressmaking aside. Never in her life had she fixed a car, mended a fuse or wallpapered a room. There had always been someone, even before her marriage, willing to help for chivalrous or more calculated motives. She had always depended, and that depending got you nowhere. In the end, you couldn't rely on anyone, not even a reliable husband like Cameron.

'That's very kind of you, but I can do it myself. I'll be in tomorrow.'

Bits of body, detached or otherwise, represented death to Rhona more than any whole corpse. The hand in the corner of the shed was more chilling than anything she had experienced since her father's accident. A hand could say so many things, and a hand that lay still seemed so very much more dead than any other part of the body except, perhaps, the head. Her panicked howl of fear was the nearest she had come to expressing her feelings so far, and Joel flinched when he heard it. She ran out of the shed and back in again. Before either of them could compose themselves the tarpaulin rustled and moved. The hand disappeared and a head emerged.

'Jesus Christ!' A young man with long black hair lay staring at them, clearly as startled by the masks of white mud as by the scream. They stared back through the holes in their face masks, motionless.

'Ah . . .' he said at last, running a hand through his greasy hair. 'Shit, you scared me.'

'Who are you?' asked Joel bravely.

'I'm just . . . I'm not . . .'

'Yes, who *are* you?' asked Rhona, still shaking, covering her flower pots modestly with her folded arms.

'I needed somewhere to kip down and . . . I thought this place was derelict. I'm sorry. Do you live here?'

'Yes. This is my house,' said Rhona, as if she paid the mortgage. 'I'm Rhona, and this is my best friend Joel.'

Joel looked pleased for a moment. No one had ever introduced him like that before. And it looked as if they were going to have a real adventure after all.

'Pleased to meet you,' said the young man, holding out the hand in question. Joel and Rhona both shook it solemnly. 'My name's . . .' he hesitated, 'Gabe – short for Gabriel.'

'So why are you here?' she continued.

'I needed to get away. I've been having some hassles with my parents. I mean, like, things were really heavy. Hey, look, you won't tell anyone I'm here, will you?'

Rhona began to smile a little. 'I'll have to consult my friend.'

She signalled to Joel to go outside the shed, and carefully closed the door behind them. She put a finger to her lips and opened her eyes very wide. 'It's him!' she whispered excitedly.

'Who?'

'Wig! It's Wig!'

'It isn't.'

'It *is*. Don't you see? He didn't want to tell us his name. That one's made up, I bet.'

'But Wig's a star. He wouldn't have parents.'

'That's just a story. He's trying to avoid publicity and stuff.'

'Well . . .' Joel looked dubious. 'I suppose he does have long black hair.'

'Exactly. And Wig is *missing*.'

'Well, if he was Wig he could play a guitar.'

'Right. Good thinking. Wait here. Whatever you do, don't let him go.'

A few minutes later they re-entered the shed.

'It's OK – it's only us,' said Rhona. She held out an old classical guitar with Woodstock and Glastonbury stickers which seemed to have become part of the wood. 'Will you play us a tune, then?'

The young man raised his eyebrows, took the guitar and examined it slowly.

'We brought you some food as well,' said Joel, emptying

Rhona's pockets for her. He held out some squashed quiche and half a packet of custard creams.

The young man smiled warmly and thanked them. He started to tune the guitar while Joel and Rhona watched anxiously.

'We know who you are!' said Rhona, unable to contain herself at last.

There was a loud twang. He looked up very nervously. 'How do you know that?'

'You're Wig from When!' Rhona gave a triumphant, exhilarated smile. 'And you can stay here as long as you like! We won't tell a soul, will we, Joel?'

Joel shook his head vigorously. Gabe looked at them both in turn, and then struck up a jagged melody on the guitar, smiling.

Routines, thought Tina, seemed to establish themselves remarkably quickly. They emerged in rough form after a couple of days, and before a week was out it was as though there had never been anything else but this particular pattern to day and night. And a week after the funeral this was the Morrisons' fully fledged routine: Rhona walked to school with Joel; Tina drove to work at Did-It-Myself on Mondays, Thursdays and Fridays, working on the house the remaining four days; Bubbles stayed at home in her granny annexe (a bed and a chair) or shopped for food, more or less following a list Tina left, but with some exciting variations from time to time; at three Tina returned from work and did an hour or so on the house; at three thirty Rhona returned from school and complained that she hated it; at midnightish Tina cried. The long silent night was punctuated only by the sound of the milk float at four.

At the checkout near the door at Did-It-Myself was a Fabseal calendar turned to May and asking, 'Would you use anything else on your wood?' As Tina ticked off the tenth she put a hand to her mouth. The fifteenth was Rhona's birthday, her eleventh, and she had completely forgotten. Rhona had talked insistently about contact lenses for the last week, and Tina had dismissed the idea as far too expensive. Only now did she realise that Rhona was hinting at her birthday. Lenses were probably still out of the question, but she would check them out. At lunchtime she slipped home and looked for Rhona's latest spectacle prescription. It was in a tea chest marked 'Files' in a file marked 'Medical'. Flicking through it she realised they had amassed every slip of paper with any remote medical connection for the past eight years. She would have to do some sorting. She found the prescription between a magazine article on the use of oats for eczema at the top of which Cameron had written 'Mum', and one on 'Elderly Primagravidae' at the top of which he had written 'Tina'. She examined the writing for a moment, trying to pick up something of Cameron from the curves of the letters, wondering if their formation betrayed any of his thoughts at the time of writing it: Tina. Tina: elderly primagravida. Tina: elderly.

'Sod you, Cameron,' she said as she drove to the town centre.

'Sod you!' she muttered as she entered SpecExpress.

The man in front of her said, 'Sod you too,' and turned back to the counter.

She discovered that a surprise present was not possible because the prescription was for spectacles and not contact lenses. Rhona would need to be examined first.

'But it's her birthday!'

'I'm sorry, but the prescription may be different.'

Then a bald man who had just poured himself a coffee behind the counter said 'Morrison . . . hmmm' in an optically qualified way, Tina thought. 'That rings a bell,' he said and rifled through a filing cabinet. 'Rhona Morrison . . . here we are.' He pulled out some card and paper. 'Came in last month. I remember now. I wasn't to tell her. I had to pretend it was for specs.'

'With her father?'

'I guess so. Anyway, here's the prescription. He hasn't been back in, yet. You can order them now if you like.'

So Cameron had it all worked out. He was going to surprise his daughter, and Tina couldn't let him down. Never mind if she had to sell something to pay for it (the car?), it was a dead man's last wish.

In the shopping mall she caught the lift with a few other shoppers. A man with a pushchair – someone's husband – pressed the 'DOOR HOLD' button with his free arm for latecomers, and seemed to take control. That was what she missed without Cameron, and she slipped passively into her former self for a few seconds as the man organised the stops.

'Third floor,' said a denim-clad girl with wide hips. He raised a questioning eyebrow at Tina.

'Pelvic floor,' she said.

He smirked awkwardly, and only his unexpected reaction made her realise what she had said. She filed out quickly with the denim girl and walked randomly into the first door: a health food shop.

She stood in front of the vitamin E and evening primrose oil and gazed into the future. No husband, no baby, no freedom. She saw herself at seventy rubbing wheatgerm oil into her wizened face, having forgotten to detoxify for years, a Happy Sausage hat or somesuch perched on her grey perm. Rhona would have left, breaking all links with her for ever, ashamed and embarrassed by her uneducated stepmother. She would be alone. Alone, except . . . Bubbles would probably still be hanging on in there, a sprightly ninety-something in a T-shirt, pottering around the kitchen but needing to be tied down and spoon fed.

A blend of Neroli, Wheatgerm and Orange Blossom oils to prevent stretch marks during pregnancy. She averted her eyes. *Folic Acid: for Would-be Mums.* She turned to face the opposite counter. *Primatabs: for an easy, invigorating menopause; BLUSHBAN: flush away hot flushes for good.*

She stood between Pregnancy and Menopause and felt stuck. She wanted to sweep her arms along both counters and send the capsules and elixirs to the floor. She wanted to smash all the childproof bottles, stamp all the tablets underfoot and skate around on the essential oils. She rounded the corner and grabbed two muesli bars in one hand and a bag of yoghurt-covered nuts in the other and dashed them to the floor. She stood shaking, shocked at what she had done. Her throat felt very dry and she stayed immobile, waiting for the response. Only her eyes moved, circling the store.

No one noticed. The woman at the cash desk carried on serving and a man with a badly hand-knitted jumper carried on examining the allergic rhinitis books on the rotating stand. She eventually went to pick them up, and replaced them with trembling hands.

She returned to work late, only to be called away again by a phone call from the police. Keith Pooley eyed her anxiously as he watched her grab her cardigan and dive through the automatic doors so fast they almost didn't open in time. Had he been too hasty in appointing a woman who was late from lunch and had phone calls from the police?

Bubbles had been mugged on the way to the Co-op. The mugger had taken her purse and a quarter-pound of ham.

'The postman ran after him – some little truant from school if you ask me,' said Mavis at the Co-op store, 'but he was too fast.'

'Is she all right?'

'Oh, *she's* all right. Poor old postman I'm worried about. Well, he come back here, picked her up and calmed her down and that. Even phoned the police from here. Then when the police arrived she said *he'd* done it, calm as you like. Said she'd been mugged by the postman! Well, they were taking him off for questioning, but I said, now wait here, you phone Mrs Morrison and she'll put you right on this. It's been all I can do to keep them here.' She indicated a back room where Bubbles sat sandwiched between the postman and a policewoman. The postman had his head in his hands, and Bubbles was patting him sympathetically: 'Don't worry, dear. I'm sure they won't be too hard on you.' Then she saw Tina and explained how she had been brutally attacked by the postman: 'I was brutally attacked by the postman.'

Tina sighed and apologised to all concerned. Then she took Bubbles' sleeve in one hand and her zip-up shopping bag in the other and led her away, Bubbles turning to wave as she exited: 'I could've *given* you some ham if you'd asked me.'

As they walked up the road towards home, Bubbles snorted and suddenly spat on the pavement. Tina winced. 'Do you have to?'

'Listen,' said Bubbles, 'I know I'm forgetful nowadays, but I remember a lot of things too. I remember I used to have to walk with a bible on my head to keep a straight back and wear a hat in the street and use knives and forks from the outside in and never put an elbow on the table or speak to my elders and betters and *now,*' she paused for breath, 'now I'll spit if I want to, and bugger it!'

Rhona eyed her grandmother's shopping bag on the kitchen table. It was one of those old-fashioned, zip-up kinds that sat on a square base. This was a roomy beige PVC one with a shiny nose-like lock at the end of the zipper. It always reminded Rhona of a small dog, and she was convinced it would go to heel if Bubbles whistled. Its handles flopped down like ears, and it seemed to be sitting pathetically while Tina recounted the shameful escapade.

'Why is she always buying ham?' said Rhona. She opened the shopping bag and found more ham – four packs of it. Bubbles had been buying ham for years (it had signalled the start of her senility), so much so that Rhona thought handbags were originally for storing ham. She only discovered her mistake when an infant teacher circled her spelling of 'hambag' in red biro.

Rhona's real interest in the shopping was to see if there was anything she could safely steal for Wig – or Gabe, as she would have to remember to call him. She and Joel had fed him fairly well for a day or so, although in their excitement they had forgotten to give him anything to drink. She was concerned also about the lack of bathroom facilities, and slipped him a key to get into the house in the daytime when everyone was out. She would go to the bathroom in a moment and look for signs of him. A smudge on the towel, perhaps, or a footprint in the bath. Rhona would lie awake at night imagining scenes between her and Wig in the shed. Once she told him how uncomfortable the house was, and he told her not to go back there but to stay in the shed with him. This involved an elaborate sub-plot where she found some excuse to sneak back to the house, shower, brush her teeth and put on her Yardley's toilet scent – or some of her mother's Chanel if the coast was clear. It also posed the problem of toilets. She would get as far as the first kiss, all tender and cosy, snuggling under the tarpaulin (now lined with a soft woollen blanket and winceyette sheets which she would've provided) when the need for a toilet pressed in on her story. She would nudge it away, but it kept coming back, until she was forced to deal with it. The need for accurate detail in these fantasies was paramount, for some reason. But these nagging problems took her off at such tangents that she was usually sound asleep before the good bits.

All this commotion over Bubbles made Rhona pretty sure that her birthday had been forgotten. She knew she wouldn't get contact lenses, but what she wanted second most was a minidress from Miss Selfridge and what she wanted third most was a pair of Reebok trainers. There was no point in asking for either. She would receive a hand-made minidress (beautifully made, a superb copy, but not *quite* the same), or a pair of trainers that would look just the same, but they would be plastic, not leather. Tina never thought these details mattered. The skirt material wouldn't swirl properly and the shoe fastener wouldn't be Velcro. Rhona felt very strongly about swirling and Velcro.

There was no point in mentioning these things to her mother, who in any case had probably forgotten the date. Rhona fantasised that she had. She would wake up on her birthday and no one would say Happy Birthday. She would go down to the post on the mat and no one would have sent her a card. She would go to breakfast with a hurt look on her face and Tina would be bewildered. Joel would wonder why she was so distant on the way to school, and when she could bear it no more a teacher would brush away her tears and be appalled that an eleven-year-old had been forgotten on her birthday. When she got home the penny would drop, and Tina would hug her to pieces and take her to McDonald's for a week to make up for it. She would buy her the Miss Selfridge dress and the trainers and the contact lenses and throw her a party, and everyone at school would feel so sorry for her they would turn up with presents. Even Bubbles would give her ham or something. She surprised herself by thinking about such things at a time of mourning, but she did think about them. She wanted presents – she needed them. Or rather, she *deserved* them. She felt somehow that she deserved compensation for her father's death and people should just see that. People should treat her better, now that she was hurt.

She embroidered another scene in which Wig picked her up from school. It was perfect. Kelly Porter and Hayley Farrow were busy telling her she couldn't be in their gang because she was boring and wore plastic trainers, when Wig arrived casually and stood at the school gate, smiling. They started to scream and whimper and run towards him, while other girls dropped their tuck boxes, deserted their mothers and began to mob him. But he simply smiled and said, 'Rhona, you ready?' and she sauntered over, looking cool as a cucumber as he took her lunch box and put an arm around her. 'I need your opinion on my latest album cover – have you got time before tea?'

Jade Green

That weekend Tina spent all her free time on Rhona's room, working through mealtimes to finish some plastering. She arranged for Rhona to spend two nights at the Ferabees' on the pretext that she would be using some toxic spray. Ordinarily she felt that love expanded and contracted like a piece of elastic to suit the demands made upon it. Now she wasn't so sure. With Cameron dead and no baby, it was as though there were a great store of it, unused, bursting out of her. When she wasn't feeling angry, she wondered if her anger weren't simply displaced love. At any rate she moved around Rhona's room with a sort of reverence, touching her things affectionately as though she were the most precious person in the world to her. And probably she was.

She wore a spacious blue overall with room for another small person, and a dust mask which looked like the muzzle of some giant insect. The heat made the mask sweaty, and her own breath seemed to scorch her face. Everything was taking a lot longer than she'd expected. How could Cameron possibly have finished all this in eight weeks? He always was too ambitious, and prone to exaggeration. She had a curious feeling of contentment at the thought that he had miscalculated. Even if he had lived, they would still be panicking about sleeping with mould and cement. She didn't dwell too long on it, afraid that if she delved too deeply she might uncover an anger which was revenge for his abandoning her. She wanted him intact, the man she had dreamed with for so many years. She tried to remember what his exact last words were. The embrace in the hall, that was their last long conversation, but there had been words the following day, just before she took Bubbles to the assessment centre. Was it 'love you' or 'see you'? It seemed to her if she could just remember his last words to her they might be significant. She pictured him out the back, preparing for the afternoon's work. He pottered around in a faded T-shirt, dark springy hair, his banter a string of one-liners. He'd painted the letter x on her bare shoulder and said, 'Lots of those for you when you get back.' Then he blew on his mother's nose and sang, 'I'm forever blowing Bubbles,' as usual. Had he kissed her then? They did kiss a lot. Tina considered that one of the best features of their marriage. She remembered their first kiss, a soft nibble on the nape of the neck. He had called into the Happy Sausage with Rhona one rain-sodden day, and she thought he was just another of those divorced men who trawl their children around on Saturdays and stuff them with French fries. He ordered one strawberry and one chocolate milkshake, and she told him there was a minimum charge of three pounds between twelve and two on weekends. He offered the extra one pound twenty, but she said that was no good. He bought a plate of soggy chips and looked at them with disgust when she put them on the table, but Rhona, who was two then, squashed handfuls of them in her fists until the potato squelched out, polished off the remaining ones and squirted tomato ketchup in the sugar bowl. If he hadn't been consulting Tina about directions to somewhere or other he would probably have lectured his two-year-old on the dangers of cholesterol and E numbers. He liked his milkshake, though. Odd, now, to think he would touch anything he hadn't made himself. But he came back for another one the following week, and the week after. One week he turned up without Rhona and Tina was doing the dishes. Dawn, a wraith-like girl who worked on tables with her, came running into the kitchen and reported that he was disappointed not to see her. He stayed until closing time, sitting alone over endless milkshakes and reading his credit cards as if there were novels written on them. Dawn showed him into the kitchen and he crept up behind Tina at the sink.

'That the chocolate milkshake man?' she asked steadily as two arms stole around her waist. 'Got a complaint?'

'Yes. The service wasn't quite as good today.' And that's when he'd kissed her neck. Dead romantic. It fizzed up and down her spine and she was utterly his for ever. Remarkable now, to think of it, that someone could lay claim to you for life in such a simple manner. She could still smell the lemony scent of the washing-up liquid, feel the steam come up from the bubbles, see the tiles by the taps flecked with grease. Ah! That was it!

She was shutting the back door when she asked if he wanted anything in town.

'Don't forget the grouting!' he shouted.

'Anything else?'

'Just Readimix grout.'

Those had been his last words ever to her: *Readimix grout*.

Tina surveyed her lunchtime's work. There were only a few inches of plastering left to do in Rhona's room, and she could do that this evening. It wouldn't be decorated for her birthday, but it would be clean and vacuumed, and she would be able to put the furniture in place properly. She went to the bathroom and wrestled for a few seconds in silent combat with her overall, which seemed to defy the act of urinating. When eventually she managed to seat herself, a strange man walked in through the open door and stared at her.

'Christ!' he said, taking in the masked woman sporting canvas gloves on the toilet. He backed out quickly. She waddled after him, her knickers and overall tying her feet together so that she made slow, robotic progress to the head of the stairs.

'Who the hell are you?' she shouted, but it came out as a mumble inside the plastic mask. She waited several minutes, shaking, but he had gone. Turning, she saw that the sleeves and body of her overall had polished a trail in the dusty floor, and she stood for a moment, trying to remember what she had been doing before the interruption.

'I only wanted a shave,' said Gabriel. 'But that was a very close shave – she definitely saw me.'

'Did she see where you went?' asked Rhona, handing over a crumpled sandwich and half a doughnut, the remains of tea at Joel's.

'I don't think so. I didn't come back to the shed.'

Joel was the chief food provider lately, since Rhona's household seemed to be on rations of ham. He proudly opened a carrier bag and watched Gabriel pull out a thermos flask of tea, a scotch egg and an apple.

'Thanks, mate. Listen, you couldn't get me any fags, could you?'

'But you don't smoke,' said Rhona.

'Ah . . . well . . .'

Joel shot her a knowing glance which she caught in the corner of her eye and ignored.

'You're always saying you don't smoke – it said it in *NME*.'

'Well, I did give it up for a long time. Yes.'

'"*I can honestly say I've never touched a cigarette in all my life.*" That's what you said.'

'I did. I did say something like that. But it was a bit of a publicity stunt, you know? It's kind of nerve-racking being cooped up like this, on the run. Know what I mean? I'm getting kind of anxious. I just need something to calm my nerves.'

'Oh, I see. You're afraid at night here, all on your own.'

'Yeah. I am as a matter of fact. A fag or two would really help.'

Rhona twisted round at the waist back and forth and swung her arms to the left and right as though they were no longer strictly attached to her. 'I've got an idea,' she said, still swinging. 'My room isn't decorated or anything yet, and there are great holes in the wall, and I get scared too. If you like, I could come and keep you company.'

Joel looked indignant. 'But you can't do that!'

She turned to face him now. She had bunched her hair into what would on anyone else have been called a ponytail, but which looked on Rhona like a pom-pom stuck to her head, he thought. She pushed her glasses up her nose and looked very serious. 'Why not? I can if I want to.'

'But he's a man. You're a woman.'

Rhona waited a while for his description to seep through every part of her, and felt all warm and tingly as she repeated it in her head. Woman. Then she said brusquely, 'So?'

'But we haven't discussed it or anythink,' he said, looking hurt and panic-stricken. He hadn't considered it before, but now that he did, he considered Rhona to be his girlfriend.

'Hey, hey, hey!' interrupted Gabriel. 'I think I can sort this one out. It's very kind of you, Rhona, but I've got enough on my plate without being done for abducting little girls . . .'

Little girls! Rhona shrank visibly. She pulled Joel out of the shed roughly. 'Now look what you've done!'

Joel looked at her red, ruptured expression and then at his shoes. They were a size four from Saxone and scuffed at the toes. He didn't understand women at all.

On Monday Tina looked obliquely at customers as she made their tiles and sanders bleep at the checkout. She was planning a special birthday tea in her head, pondering sausage rolls, going-home presents and jelly.

During her lunch hour she slipped into town and visited the nearest supermarket. She tossed things into her trolley with a speedy abandon, aware that she was overspending but determined to throw the best party ever. She stood near the lift to the shopping arcade car park and consulted her list. To her left was a woman with a baby in a sling.

She ached for a baby. She looked at babies in prams and pushchairs, sometimes with a heart-melted smile, sometimes with a wistful stare of pain and longing. Spotting her, their mothers returned to tuck them in protectively or scooped them up in their arms away from her tormented face. If these women kept their babies away from her in case she snatched them, her sisters kept their babies away in case it hurt too much to see them. But none of them understood this simple fact: she didn't want *their* babies, with their squashed mouths and their ugly snouts, she wanted *her* baby: the baby whose smile would make her move heaven and earth, whose breathing would keep her awake all night in gratitude, whose gurgling she could make out from a sea of babies, whose smell made her quiver with love, whose damp nuzzling head would make her cry with joy.

To her right was the window of a fashion shop. Two little girls of about Rhona's age were eying up a dress on display. She looked at them standing there, smiling and chatting. They struck Tina as so happily normal: unremarkable. What was it about Rhona? Had she herself been remiss as a mother? Had she failed to notice the fashion trends? Not invited her friends around enough? Had she created a freak, a girl who couldn't merge into a crowd of her own age-group, because of her own inadequate mothering? She looked at the dress, a blood-red mini with threads attached to its hem, pulling it out like tent ropes to show off the skirt. The model had no head, and Tina tried to picture Rhona's on the stump. It was all she could do to refrain from rushing in and buying it, but caution got the better of her as she glanced at the load in her trolley.

After work she coasted the pavements outside Rhona's primary school ten minutes before the bell. She approached women she had never met before and asked them, 'Is your son or daughter in year six?' If they were, she issued them with a hastily written invitation decorated with balloons, and added that her daughter's party was a surprise, so as not to give the game away. Three women were standing together with an assortment of younger offspring and buggies. They looked Tina up and down with curiosity.

'So you're Mrs Morrison? I'm *so* sorry to hear about your husband,' said one of them, a tall woman whose silk clothes billowed around her slender form. Tina took in the perfectly cut blonde hair, the delicately frosted nails and the softest jade green cashmere cardigan rolled up at the sleeves. She watched the neat rows of gold hairs on the arms glint in the sunshine and said, 'Yes. Thank you.' She wanted to continue the conversation but felt cowed and tongue-tied by their easy stateliness. The woman to her right had her eye firmly fixed on Tina's Did-It-Myself embroidered pocket; she fingered a diamond the size of an aspirin on her hand and delved it into her baby's pram, where she disappeared for a moment under a frilly sun canopy.

'That's a beautiful quilt,' said Tina, spotting the delicate crochet work in the pram. 'Did you make it yourself?'

'Yes.' The woman barely surfaced.

'Did it take you long, then?'

'A yeah.'

'Yeah? How long?' asked Tina, unaware that this woman's husband's status prevented her from pronouncing her vowel sounds properly.

'A yeah.'

Tina nodded, confused. 'Oh well, then. Yeah.' She rocked back and forward on the balls of her feet, nodding.

'I thought your husband was a solicitor,' said the silk woman.

'He is – was. That's right,' said Tina, getting the picture slowly. 'But hey! A woman's got to work too, hasn't she?' She looked down at her uniform and smiled. 'Now he's gone, things are a little difficult.'

The third woman was scratching her nose and brushing a hand across her face, as if Tina were some irritant fly. She ignored Tina and turned to speak to the woman with the pram. Tina stood awkwardly, one foot on the pavement, one off. She could hear her own strong local accent and her last unanswered words seemed to hang thickly in the air like a flopped joke.

'Do you work?' she asked the silk woman.

The manicured hand went up to stroke the hair. 'I'm a councillor.'

'Oh. That must be interesting.' The woman smiled silently, and Tina began to feel she was conducting an interview. 'Must be depressing – all those broken marriages and things.'

The woman threw back her head and laughed politely. 'Gosh, no. I'm a town councillor. Erica Boreham-Green.' She paused, and then held out her hand. Tina shook it.

'Oh, right. So you don't have a proper job, then?' Tina noticed the other two women smirking at each other with the slightest curve of their mouths, but still not looking at her.

'I suppose not.'

The school bell rang and Tina hurriedly offered them all invitations. She gave out ten in all. That seemed about right. The kitchen would be a squash, but it would be worth it to see Rhona smile.

'If you ask me,' said Joel, 'there's something fishy about this Wig bloke.'

They were sitting on the low branch of a willow tree in a field near the church.

'Well, no one is asking you,' said Rhona. She was carving her initials into the tree ineptly with a blunt stick. It barely scratched the bark, and left 'RM+WIG' in a set of skid marks.

'But I think he could be dangerous.'

'You're only jealous.'

'Why should I be?'

'Because I'm in love with him and I'm going to seduce him.'

Joel swallowed. 'You can't.'

'Why not?'

'He's too old, and I won't let you.'

'Well, stop me then.' Rhona smiled. 'I'm going to seduce him tomorrow after school, before Mum gets back. You're not invited.'

'You can't. Your mum said you have to stay at our place after school. She told me to make sure you were with me.'

'No she didn't.'

'She did. She said she didn't want to frighten you, but there was a strange man lurking around – he went into your bathroom yesterday and she saw him. She made me *promise* not to take my eyes off you for a moment.'

'Well, that's OK. You can watch.'

He scratched his freckled nose defensively. 'Well anyway, I think he really is dangerous. My mum said she saw a strange man lurking around your house when your dad died.'

Rhona looked up quickly. Joel glanced off to the side to avoid meeting her sharp eyes.

'You're only saying that now because you don't like him suddenly.'

'I'm not. It's true. I didn't tell you before because I only heard yesterday, and anyway I thought he was Wig too but now I don't.'

'What are you saying? That he killed Dad?'

'No. Well . . .' Joel was floored by this. He was hoping it might make her suspicious at least, but he wasn't expecting such hostility.

'Dad fell off a ladder, and you're just trying to spoil everything for me, as if my life wasn't bad enough!'

'He didn't! Mum said he suffocated. Your mum doesn't want anyone to know. I heard her telling Dad on the landing . . .'

He was expecting some sort of recognition for this information, and he opened his eyes wide in anticipation of her curiosity. But Rhona swung from the tree and ran, leaving him astride the bough with his back to her. He twisted his head and called after her.

'Don't shout at me!' she screamed.

Joel thought about this one. He spoke her name instead, but it didn't seem to reach her.

Tina sat coyly in the kitchen, waiting for a reaction to the bedroom.

'God!' shrieked Rhona as she came down the stairs. 'You've changed everything!'

Tina smiled bashfully. 'Do you like it?'

Rhona shot into the kitchen and seemed to reel around like a drunkard.

'No! You've changed all the furniture round!'

'Well, we can always—'

'Why didn't you ask me? *I* wanted to do my bedroom. Why did you have to do that!'

'You don't like it, then?'

'Got it in one!'

Tina felt a slight difficulty swallowing. Rhona wasn't a spoilt child and she seemed to have genuinely upset her quite by mistake.

'I thought it would be a nice surprise for you.'

'I hate it. I hate it! Now it'll stay like that for ever because we haven't got a man to move it around.'

Tina shifted awkwardly in her chair, fumbling with a pile of birthday cake candles which she was trying to conceal on her lap.

Rhona ran back upstairs and burst into tears on her bed. The sun was low and casting diagonal yellow bands across the newly plastered walls. She felt churned up by her own behaviour. She could see that her mother had spent a good deal of time on the room, and not one of the other rooms had any new plastering yet. She wasn't going to be grateful, though. She *deserved* special treatment. If her father had been alive he would have done the same without even thinking about it. Then it occurred to her that Tina had not, in fact, made any ceremony over it. She had done it as a surprise, not to score any points. She was probably sitting in the kitchen right now, wondering why she'd bothered, thinking what a spoilt child Rhona was and deciding not to look after her at all any more, now that she didn't really have to. She followed the bands of sunlight and her eyes fell on something stuck to the wardrobe. She stood up and approached slowly. There, Blu-tacked on to the doors, were two pictures of Wig cut from a magazine, and a picture of a baby seal. She hadn't seen any of them before; they weren't from her collection. Tina had found them, cut them out, stuck them up. There was something about the combination of pictures which tore at Rhona's heart. She was confused by the feeling. The pop star seemed evidence of her mother's respect for imminent adolescence. The seal was a childish picture, but it looked at Rhona with such sad wide eyes it seemed to display a vulnerability which she herself felt and which Tina understood. She pictured her mother cutting them out carefully, anticipating her delight. She turned over and cried. It felt like a different kind of crying to anything that had come before. Hotter and deeper, even, than any tears she had cried for her father. It was a complicated, bewildering feeling. She was, for the first time, crying for someone else's hurt.

The sounds of a summer night slowly faded. Crockery stopped clacking and conversations heard through windows trailed off. As people called their dogs in and lights went out in Church Road, Gabriel crept in through the back door of the house. He needed the bathroom urgently. He thought all the lights were off downstairs, but when he had picked his way carefully to the foot of the stairs he stopped, listened, and turned back. There was a glow of light from one of the rooms and a whirring noise. It sounded like a sewing machine.

Beige Sorcery

'Like I said, your living room's all right, look,' said Keith Pooley the following morning. He had called round on his way to work to ask if Tina could cover a few hours for another cashier, and to deliver some equipment. He couldn't resist another look at the work in hand. 'You got the new boards all ready to go down – don't know what you had there – bit of wet rot I shouldn't doubt. No sign of it now. But you got a bit of a tide mark on the wall.'

'Oh.' Tina was determined to follow every word.

He knelt down with the magnificent mechanism of his folding legs and swept his competent hand across a lower portion of wall. 'Bit of rising damp – usually caused by lack of damp proof course. See, they weren't compulsory till 1875, and I reckon this house goes back . . . ooh . . . dunno . . . older than that, at any rate.'

'So I haven't got one, then?'

'Oh, I'm not saying that, look. Your old stone's all right, actually. It's these rendered brick walls. I reckon your problem's just that bit of garden outside the front window – or patio thingy, whatever – he's gone and bridged the damp proof course.'

'It's the sand! There's a big pile of sand outside the front against the wall.' She was getting the hang of this.

'There you go, then. All you've got to do is strip any earth or whatnot away from the wall above that level, and then you'll need a dehumidifier inside. I got you a couple on loan, look. And you might need to do a bit of replastering.'

She nodded and followed as he rose elegantly, drifted into the hallway and leant with one arm on the banister. She noticed that his eyes were a very deep blue, and matched his uniform.

'Also, you got penetrating damp in your bedrooms and dining room. That's going to need a bit of detective work, but I'd bet on it being your leaky roof and possibly some cracked rendering outside – though it does look quite good. You'll have to check that.'

She was fascinated by his expertise, but felt herself slipping into dependency. 'Have you got any manuals?'

'What? Still fancy doing it yourself, do you? Yes, I've got no end of manuals.'

He had brought two dehumidifiers in his pick-up truck and a box of DIY manuals. He spent half an hour explaining the contents of one of them.

As he left her to go to work, Keith Pooley felt a sense of cheer which he couldn't attribute to anything in particular. He was always pleased to put his skills to good use, and he was certainly pleased to know the inhabitants of number twenty-three. The house had been empty for some time, but before that it had been lived in by a wealthy old lady from Poole who kept herself and her grounds to herself. Until this past month he couldn't remember when he had last heard children's high-pitched voices echoing in its gardens.

Keith Pooley was the sort of person who liked to know his patch. He wasn't one of those people who travelled round the world and knew a bit of everything superficially. He liked to study a small part of it in depth. He knew every tree in Moorhampton and the blooming time of every plant and shrub. He knew when the first crocuses would be out up by the church, and he waited with certainty for the appearance of those in his garden three days later, where there was just that bit less sun. He knew from the length of the summer which week in August or September the first blackberries would appear. He knew all the faces of the children erupting from the primary school at three thirty on his afternoon off. He saw in each one the features of parents he had swapped conkers with or kissed in a game of tag.

Linda had hated him for his small town mentality. She wanted to see the world, to travel to Paris and Rome and live in a house in London where their parents would rarely visit them. She wanted to re-create a world for herself, a different one, but one in which she widened her circle of friends indefinitely. To her there was so much more to life than Moorhampton: so much to be learnt, so many, many people to meet and places to go. It was all out there waiting to be found. But Keith saw her wanting to cram too much in. All she did was brush the surface of everything. She wasn't interested in depth. As far as he could see, there was only so much time in life. You had a fixed amount of it to find out all there was to know. You could search wildly, and spend all your time travelling and skirting past things, or you could stay where you were and burrow deeply. He was a burrower. In any case, people were probably much the same the world over. He knew everything there was to know about Moorhampton, but there were still constant surprises. For example, he hadn't known Tina Morrison. Her shapely mouth and translucent teeth seemed to smile at him long after he had gone. He liked her quietness, and the promise – tied up in her ribbon – of cascading hair, and he liked the softness of her shape, the lack of angularity.

If you stayed long enough in one place, people came to you.

Going-home presents. She didn't have any. As soon as her cover at work was finished, Tina took Bubbles into town and walked urgently in and out of shops. Then she spotted some Teddy-shaped balloons on huge cardboard feet swaying in a toyshop window. She steered Bubbles through the doorway and asked for eleven. Perfect. She looked around to find Bubbles examining a furry, battery-operated elephant, which raised its trunk and hooted every five seconds. Tina scanned her for signs of trouble, but Bubbles was quite lucid and cheerful.

As they hurried towards the bus stop, Bubbles stopped. 'My bag!' It was not on her arm nor on the pavement behind them. Tina tried not to sigh.

'Where did you leave it?'

'Oh, perhaps I left it at home.'

'No, you had it.'

'Did I?'

'You had it in the toyshop.'

'Oh! I believe I did.'

'Have you put it down somewhere?'

'Have I? Well, goodness, that was silly! Shall we go back and look for it?' Even as she spoke she was turning, making for her lost bag like a homing pigeon. Tina put her arm out and stopped her.

'No! I'll go.' She placed both hands on Bubbles' shoulders and said, '*Stay here*.'

They were standing outside the town hall, and it seemed a good place to leave a woman who became lost on a daily basis. Even so, Tina drew from her own bag a small Did-It-Myself clipboard with her shopping list on it and wrote her address and telephone number in large letters. She gave it to Bubbles and said, 'Show this to someone if you get lost, OK?'

'I know where I live,' said Bubbles with contempt.

'I won't be long. Just *stay here*.'

Tina ran nervously back down the four streets to the toyshop, colliding with small children, pushchairs and a band of Japanese tourists, all the while wondering how she would cope with her mother-in-law indefinitely. Fortunately the beige bag was sitting obediently by the counter, and contained no items of stolen property. As she picked it up, smiling with relief at the young woman assistant, she noticed a musical mobile with soft satin penguins which bounded around, curiously, to 'How Much is that Doggie in the Window?' It hadn't been playing before, and now she was enthralled.

'It's for a baby's cot,' said the assistant. 'Reduced to fourteen pounds ninety-nine. Got the wrong tune, see. You won't find better value than that, though.'

Tina rummaged for her purse, folded her lips into her teeth, and decided to be extravagant. There was no harm in it.

As she neared the elegant columns of the town hall, she could see no sign of the small lady in the beige raincoat she had left there. It was busy, so she wandered around, raising herself on her toes now and then to see if Bubbles were behind a tall man. But she was not where Tina had left her with the clipboard, and nowhere in sight. In the distance, she saw the number seven bus stop with a long tail of passengers, and wondered if Bubbles was in it. She waited five minutes and then made her way slowly in that direction, looking down every street and inspecting shop doorways. The bus was already arriving and she began to speed up. The entire pavement seemed suddenly blocked by a crowd of people and, taking a wide detour into the road, she noticed they were the Japanese tourists she had encountered earlier near the town hall. Their tour guide had allowed them to obstruct the whole pavement, forcing Tina off the kerb, nearly hitting a cyclist. They were a picture of concentration, craning to listen to their guide: 'This is the cinema,' Bubbles was saying, and twenty-four faces turned up to look at the sign saying 'ODEON'. 'It dates from the nineteen twenties, and generations of Moorhamptonians have begun their courtship in these very seats.' Tina stared, but Bubbles was in her stride. 'And down here we have Miss Selfridge—'

'Bubbles!'

Bubbles smiled radiantly. 'Hello! Would you like to join us? We're going to Miss Selfridge.'

'No, you're not!' She yanked Bubbles by the elbow and tugged her through the posse of tourists. 'You're coming home with me!'

A smiling Japanese man in a beautifully tailored coat tapped her on the shoulder: 'Pweese. We see Miss Seffwidge now?'

Tina found him too courteous to cold-shoulder. 'I'm sorry,' she said. 'The tour's over now. Miss Selfridge is down here. I'll show you.'

When at last they arrived at the bus stop, they met Mrs Ferabee.

'I just popped down town to change a dress and – would you believe it? – they've no more in! Mother-in-law all right?'

'Finding it a bit hard to think straight just now,' said Tina, as two dozen Japanese tourists emerged from Miss Selfridge and waved at Bubbles, thanking her in turn.

They said it wasn't Alzheimer's for sure; maybe just an early dementia. When she was married Bubbles had trodden on egg-shells, tiptoed around her husband trying to defuse explosive situations. She had taken Cameron and her youngest, Alistair, to the safe haven of a hippie commune for many years, but returned after a begging phone call, asking her to help him dry out. Strength and resolve seemed to leak out of her like air from a balloon when she thought he needed her. But her forgetfulness always provoked his anger. At that time she was just embarrassed by it, mortified if she forgot to turn the oven on or found herself in a field unable to find her way home. Soon she was living in a state of constant shame and fear, punished by bruises and violent rages. She knew she was losing her mind, and if she forgot, he reminded her. He ridiculed her in public and snapped in private. The commune had disbanded, and she felt quite listless and alone. She wrote her name and address on her hand and instructions to herself around the house. Some days she found herself in a strange place, littered with notices in her own handwriting saying 'Put lunch in oven at 12.00' and 'Turn oven ON', or 'YOU LIVE HERE' when she felt certain, somehow, that she did not.

But now everything was different. As the years passed after her husband's death, she no longer noticed she was ill. No one reminded her, and she felt she had been set loose on a world of possibilities. She could speak with total strangers and wander through unknown gardens and buildings with nothing more than an accepting sigh from Tina at the end of her adventure. She felt released. She forgot to be embarrassed, and if she could have explained it, she might have said that she was happier now than she had ever been.

Mrs Ferabee blinked, and Bubbles smiled, producing from her pocket a bunch of notes and counting them.

'Whatever . . .?' began Tina.

' . . . one hundred and twenty, one hundred and twenty-five.' She unzipped her hold-all and plopped them in. 'Tips,' she said innocuously. 'What lovely people!'

Forest Pine

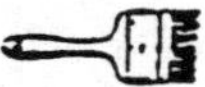

Rhona had seen it in a black and white TV film: the heroine cries on the hero's shoulder, he takes pity on her and the next thing you know he's wrapped his arms around her and, well, hey presto! She would tell him about her father's death and her being an orphan and that. (She might embroider on her real mother's death for effect, although she couldn't remember it.) Then she would say how no one loved her – not even Joel – and that she was all alone in the world. Of course she would cry, and he would have to pat her on the shoulder at the very least. And then she would lean her head against his chest and snuggle in closer, until he sort of hugged her. She would smell of Oil of Ulay and Yardley's and he would smell like a pop star (sort of fruity, she imagined). Then she would just tilt her head back a smidgen and her lips would kind of hover around his.

She sat on the back porch painting her nails in Flamenco Red. She had found an old lipstick of Tina's in a clashing cerise, and she flashed Joel a garish smile as she stood up to wave her nails dry. Joel, who was watching from the apple tree next door, had thought he was invisible. He picked at a leaf and started to hum to himself, a tune he made up as he went along, starting off nervously with something like the 'Captain Scarlet' theme tune and metamorphosing rapidly into 'There's No Business like Show Business'.

When he looked up Gabe was approaching the shed. He must have been out for a long walk, because his hair had a sodden, skinny look to it and it had not rained for over an hour. He clutched his elbows and looked cold in his sleeveless T-shirt. Joel thought he had a funny walk: he sort of lolloped along in disorganised movements as though progress were purely arbitrary. Even though he was the opposition, Joel felt a curious sympathy for him: *he* wouldn't like to be walking into a seduction trap in such an unprepared state.

A few seconds later he saw Rhona make her way to the shed door. She looked ridiculous. She minced along in a bright pink dress and heeled sling-backs he knew she had borrowed from her mother, because there was at least an inch of shoe jutting out behind her heel. With every step she sank slightly into the rain-softened grass and had to re-establish her posture. He could see her only from the back, now. The wiry hair scrunched up on top and tied with a ribbon looked like a bunch of dried flowers protruding from her head. Just before she opened the door to the shed she turned, looked directly up at the tree, and lifted the hem of her skirt to reveal dark stocking tops and suspenders. Joel looked away, hoping she would think he hadn't seen her, but he was very worried now. This Gabe bloke could be dangerous, and his girl was about to throw herself at him. She might be kidnapped or anything.

As Tina neared the gate with Bubbles she saw Joel sitting alone on the wall, swinging his legs in a lonesome fashion.

'Where's that girl of mine?' she said, smiling. He gave her an ambiguous look, she thought. 'I thought you were going to keep an eye on her for me.'

'I tried,' he said plaintively.

Now Tina was worried. 'Do you mean she's not with you? Where's your mum? Didn't she come home from school?'

Joel wasn't sure which question to answer. He had let Mrs Morrison down and he felt weak and unheroic.

'I'm worried about that strange man I saw wandering around here yesterday. You do understand, don't you? Have you seen her at all?'

'I saw her near the shed' – he saw his chance and grabbed it, without considering the consequences – 'with a strange man.'

Even as he said it he felt wicked, and as Tina marched over to the shed he wondered if he would ever be forgiven.

Tina flung open the shed door and gaped. There was that man again with his arms all round her shaking daughter. And Rhona had been dressed up to look like some sort of trollop.

'What the hell . . .?'

Rhona lifted a wet, mascara-smudged face and stopped sobbing. Her generous lipstick made her look like a drag artist or a child prostitute. She whimpered, 'Oh, Mum!'

'Who the hell are you?' screamed Tina, almost at the same time as Gabe pushed past her and shot through the door. She grabbed the nearest long-handled object – a rusty rake – and ran in raging pursuit. Rhona put her head in her hands, and then her hands over her ears to smother the shrieks that rang out down the garden.

Joel stood watching, immensely impressed as Mrs Morrison – normally so quiet – hurtled her way towards the youth screaming words he didn't know grown-ups knew. They circled the house, and as Gabriel reached the front gate he turned to say, 'Hey, look, I can explain—' But she lunged at him with the rake and he fled down the road. The lace curtains of the council house row were tugged back as a wild woman wagging a rake was heard screeching: 'Bastard! Child molester! You monster, you! You come near my daughter again and I'll—' She hurled the weapon at him and missed. He had escaped.

By now the entire street was looking on. Tina picked up the rake as though she had just happened to find it on the pavement and tried to beat a dignified retreat, clearing her throat and holding her head up high as she strode home in her Did-It-Myself uniform.

When Rhona reluctantly betrayed the secret of Gabe's true identity to her mother, she had expected at least to be believed. Banning him from their house for ever did not seem a very fitting birthday present, and she was still sulky the following morning when she came down to her birthday cards. Tina was pleased to have planned some surprises for later: perhaps by then Rhona would have calmed down. Even so, she did feel sorry for her newly eleven-year-old protégée as she watched her open the slim batch of cards on her plate (from Tina herself, Joel, a grandfather and a couple of aunts). Her friend who had moved away had forgotten. Tina remembered how quickly childhood friends were replaced when they moved away.

When she handed over the small parcel containing the contact lenses, she wanted to reassure Rhona that something else was in store, but the only clue she gave was a promise that she could open another present this evening and invite Joel to a birthday tea after school.

As the little package was opened Tina waited nervously for the reaction, afraid the rift between them was too great this morning for any gratitude. But Rhona hooted with delight and ran to the bathroom to try them on. She wasn't quite sure how to do it. She came downstairs with watering eyes and put her arms round Tina's neck.

After school Rhona was steered away from the kitchen and ran upstairs to change. She was allowed to wear her contact lenses for one hour each day initially, and she was going to put them in now and look at herself for the first time ever without glasses. She came down, blinking vigorously, to see Tina hatching a life-size pink rabbit from a blancmange mould and seating it on a table whose every inch was covered with good things to eat. She blinked in disbelief. There, floating up and down before her, were sausage rolls, fairy cakes, chocolate éclairs, cheesecakes, crustless sandwiches, pizza slices, crisps and dips of every colour. She looked at her mother whose face seemed suddenly like a question mark. It was as though this woman, who had banished her only love from the shed, had been transformed from master to slave. The eyes searched earnestly for approval, and Rhona gave it with a full-toothed smile.

The phone rang and Tina rushed to answer it. She said, 'Not to worry,' into the receiver, 'it was a bit short notice.'

Joel arrived first, clutching an enormous home-made cracker in green crêpe with curly clumps of red ribbon at each end. He looked warily at Rhona, who breathed out a long sigh and let him in. She opened it and examined three handkerchiefs with R embroidered on them in blue. It was unlikely that Joel had had anything to do with the present, she thought. She wasn't sure if he was to blame for the previous day's fiasco, but she would find out later and expel him from her party. For the meantime she thanked him, put on some music, and went to ask Tina if she could open a parcel she'd found.

Tina was on the phone. 'I see. Well, never mind. Another time, perhaps. Thanks for calling.'

'Who was that?' asked Rhona.

'No one. Nothing important.'

Rhona was carrying a large parcel crackling with brown paper. 'Can I open it?'

'It's for pass the parcel.'

'Are we having more people, then?'

Tina wasn't sure any more. She didn't want to spoil any surprises, though, so she said: 'Wait and see.'

Rhona sat in the hallway with Joel playing five- or ten-minute snatches from Wig cassettes, snapping them in and out of the tape deck like an impatient disc jockey.

'Did you get into trouble?' he asked nervously.

She shrugged. 'Mum said I looked like a prostitute.'

'Oh.'

'Do you know what a prostitute is?'

'Of course!'

'You don't!'

'I do!'

'Are you a prostitute, then?'

Joel looked at her face for clues.

'I'm not saying,' he said.

Every now and then they scurried to the kitchen table to inspect the food, or to the front window to see if a car door slamming was someone coming. An hour passed and no one else arrived. Rhona had to take her contact lenses out. The phone rang one more time, but that was all. Tina said, 'Let's go and get Bubbles. Then we can play pass the parcel with the four of us.' But when she returned with Bubbles, she found Joel with a sausage roll across his teeth and Rhona huddled in a chair, hugging her knees and gazing at the food, her eyes swimming.

'No one's coming, are they?'

Tina opened her mouth to speak, but could think of nothing appropriate to say.

'You invited lots of people to my party and no one wants to come.'

'Of course I didn't! Crumbs, we hardly *know* anyone here yet. There's plenty of time to make friends. I just thought we could have all your favourite food as a special treat.' She went over to her and folded a lock of the springy hair over her finger. 'It's not every day you're eleven, after all. Come on, pet. Why don't you open another present? Bubbles has got one for you.'

Bubbles handed her a package wrapped in silver and gold with thin ribbons dribbled all over it. Rhona looked up and took it reluctantly. Inside she unravelled a bright red minidress in a material that seemed to melt from fold to fold. She held it up and her eyebrows knitted with incredulity.

'Bubbles didn't buy this, did she?' she said at last. 'You did.'

Tina said nothing, because Rhona was already darting to her room to try it on. She spent the next quarter of an hour in front of the long mirror in Tina's room, walking up and down, admiring herself from the back with a smaller mirror, and twirling round so that the skirt spun out like the petals of a poppy. She was too enthralled to notice that there was no label.

The doorbell rang, and Tina's hopes leapt for an instant, until she saw Keith Pooley on the doorstep.

'I didn't want to interrupt or anythink,' he said. 'If now's not a convenient time, I'll just drop this off.'

He turned and went to the back of his small van which he'd parked in the drive. Tina followed him. She saw a large box-like object draped with a pink sheet; he picked it up delicately and took it into the kitchen. She padded after him.

'A little something for Rhona's birthday,' he said.

'Oh, crikey!'

Tina had to swap her feelings of mild irritation at seeing him for feelings of gratefulness and relief. She whispered, 'That's *so* kind of you. Fancy remembering . . . Won't you stay and help us eat all this food? Could you pretend I was expecting you? No one's turned up to her party.'

Keith Pooley pulled a sorry face. 'I'd be glad to. Now let me explain. I made this, but I made it for *my* daughter – so's you don't go thinking I've been working away for months specially.

Only what with her being absent from my life and so on, I thought I'd like to see it go to a good home. See, she'd be thirteen now, and I don't think she'd appreciate it no more.'

Rhona came in at this point and sashayed across the room to give Keith Pooley the full benefit of her swirling skirt. She beamed at him when she realised he had come bearing a gift, and pulled off the pink sheet with delight.

Then she stood very still. Tina chewed her cheek, praying for Rhona's gratitude, but fearfully aware that he had miscalculated her daughter's age. Keith Pooley smiled expectantly, and still Rhona stared. In front of her was a beautiful, hand-crafted doll's house.

Some seconds passed before Joel went over and unhooked the front of the house. It opened on a hinge, and he exclaimed at the intricacy of the rooms as he talked Rhona through her magical new gift. She pushed him aside by body displacement and claimed her possession. She peeked into each room like a voyeur on scenes of domesticity. In the kitchen a tiny doll with grey woollen hair was holding the smallest kettle she had ever seen, and in the living room another doll sat holding a newspaper the size of a postage stamp on a sofa whose velvet pile seemed like uncut grass around him. His clothes seemed every colour of the rainbow. She pulled him out.

'Look – his legs bend and everything!'

'I *said* that,' said Joel.

'Oh, Mr Pooley,' she breathed, turning, 'I *knew* there was someone else coming to my birthday! I knew something else was going to happen!'

'And Mr Pooley made it all himself,' said Tina, relieved.

And then, to everyone's astonishment, Rhona darted at Keith Pooley and gave him a hug. 'Thank you! *Thank you!*'

He looked winded, then smiled, 'There 'tiz.'

Everyone ate; Bubbles played her guitar; Joel and Rhona ran in and out of the garden, squabbled over the doll's house and pass the parcel, and danced wildly with Bubbles. As Rhona blew her candles out it was as though she were breathing new life into the house, each little flame being replaced by a warm giggle. Tina watched her screw up her eyes and wish.

At nine thirty Mrs Ferabee came to collect her protesting son, and Keith Pooley made a polite exit. Tina and Rhona left Bubbles washing up in the kitchen and went to look at the stars. They sat on the step outside the French window and let their heads drop back to take in the whole sky.

'It's been a lovely birthday, in the end,' said Rhona, leaning her head on Tina's shoulder. Tina smelt of baking and talcum powder, and she felt safe. 'Can I ask you something?'

'Of course.'

'Is it true that Dad was stifled?'

She had meant to say 'suffocated', but the word somehow eluded her, and the two words seemed pretty much synonymous anyway.

'Stifled?'

'Yes. Mrs Ferabee told Joel Dad was stifled.'

Tina swallowed. She felt her stomach churn. Had she stifled him? Maybe she had pressed too hard for a child of their own. Maybe he had wanted to get out more, live a bit after his degree. Had she overwhelmed him with responsibilities too suddenly? At thirty-nine? Had he told *Mrs Ferabee*? Had everyone been aware of his burdensome wife except her?

'I didn't think he was. Do you think so?'

'No, no. Joel says daft things sometimes.' She focused on a star. 'Make a wish.'

Tina looked up at the display in the sky and marvelled at the compact dimensions of human affection. Of all the cafés on all the planets in all the heavens, Cameron had walked into hers, and she had looked no further than the end of her arms for love ever since.

She wished she could turn the clocks back so that she could ask him if he was stifled or not. She wished that by some fluke she were carrying his child.

'What did *you* wish?' she asked Rhona.

Rhona looked up at her. 'You're not going to leave me, are you?'

'Why ever should I do that?'

'Now that I'm an orphan, and everything. I suppose you've no need to stay with Bubbles and me. We're just dragging you down. Why would you want to stay with us now that Dad's gone?'

'*Because,* Miss Moffat . . .' she used the name she used to call her as a toddler, and kissed the top of her head, 'I've no intention of leaving my grumpy little friend.'

Rhona nuzzled in closer. 'That's what I wished for.'

'What about your cake? Did you make a wish on the candles?'

Rhona looked wistful, and dug some icing out of her nails. 'I wished for a daddy.'

A band of cloud started to steal across the stars. A motorbike buzzed past through the quiet evening, leaving a silence which seemed to press down on both of them.

Eventually Tina heard a gentle sniffing, and felt a tear on her neck. She pulled Rhona closer to her.

'That's one wish I can't do anything about, sweetheart.'

Rhona started to sob. Soon she was choking for breath, snorting and wailing so loudly that she had to bury her face in Tina's lap so as not to frighten herself. Tina felt a certain relief. Rhona had suppressed her grief for so long that this could only be healthy. She stroked Rhona's hair and cried silently with her.

Half an hour passed and Rhona suddenly lifted her head with a look of defiance.

'You *could* do something about it! You *could*! You could find another husband instead of messing around with the house all the time and then we'd be a proper family again and we could afford things like everyone else!'

She pulled away and ran for the stairs, leaving Tina aghast.

Rhona headed for her bedroom, and then changed her mind. Tina would only follow her and she would have to explain herself. She wanted to wallow in uninterrupted misery for several more hours yet. She flew into an unused spare room and slammed the door.

She blinked. It was as though she had been transferred to another planet. A swarm of short, multi-coloured aliens swayed around on the bed. On closer inspection they were balloon bears, smiling gormlessly at her as they bobbed to and fro on their giant cardboard feet in the draught from the door. She frowned at them. They smiled back. Each set of feet were the shape of Teddy paws with 'NAME:____' on them. Each gap had been filled with a name in Tina's hand. And the funny thing was, lots of them seemed to be names of people in her class.

Baby Blue

When Tina went back into the kitchen she found Bubbles bundling the remaining food into her beige shopping bag, for reasons best known to herself.

'What are you doing?'

'I'm packing some up for Cameron. It was such a shame he couldn't be here.'

Indeed.

Tina flopped down at the table and watched her mother-in-law buzzing around more perkily than she had seen her for some time. Her blonde perm was growing out, and by now was long and crinkly with grey at the roots. It fell into a centre parting, which reminded Tina that Bubbles had been, by all accounts, quite a star in the sixties and seventies. Cameron once said that he had lived in a commune with her for many years while they waited vainly for his father to 'dry out'. The commune was in an old manor next door to a Gloucestershire vicarage. It was set up by two lesbian hippies and consisted of fourteen gentle people who put flowers in their hair and all played zithers, badly. She had sung unaccompanied in folk clubs around the region and soon gained quite a name for herself nationally. Then she took up the guitar and made an LP: *The Seeds of Love*. They had a copy somewhere. Bubbles appeared on the sleeve astride a country stile, the tips of dainty black boots appearing under a long patchwork skirt. She must have been in her late thirties – Tina's age – but she gave the impression of a rosy-cheeked child. When you opened the album cover her face appeared larger than life as a double page spread. Her woolly red hair filled most of the picture, and her clear green eyes peered out tenderly from the two sheaves that sprouted on either side of the centre parting. Her skin was peachy: that warm, cinnamon glow that only redheads seemed to have. Around her neck was a black velvet choker, and her throat was smooth and snowy.

Tina looked over at Bubbles who was singing to herself by the sink: she was still a striking woman in her mid-sixties. Large speckles like cornflakes now stained her hands and arms, and soft flesh pulled at her jowls. But the set of the jaw, the curve of the cheek and the still generous eyelids gave her a languid, only just neglected beauty. And she hadn't simply been a folk star. Cameron told of her mystic and healing skills too. People came from far and wide to be healed, it seemed, since the vicar's sick son, Ivan, had got up and walked after one of her herbal teas (although Cameron reckoned this was owing to its urgent impact on Ivan's bowels).

It was hard to imagine that this fiery woman still inhabited the person pottering about now with the clingfilm.

Tina must have dozed off, because she was woken by the sound of tapping on the French windows. She had dreamt she was a roll of carpet lying in the hall, waiting to be unravelled. Looking up she saw Bubbles through the glass, pink-cheeked and smiling. It was eleven thirty.

As Tina opened the glass door Bubbles floated in with a waft of cool night air and musk and her zip-up bag.

'No, no – don't shut the door! I've brought Cameron back.'

'Cameron?'

Tina looked out and saw Gabriel on the patio.

'*You!* You've got a nerve!'

'Bubbles said you wanted to see me—'

'Who the hell *are* you?'

He held up his hands in front of him, as though in a hold-up. 'Whoa there! Easy mistake. I'm sorry. I'll be off.'

'Oh no you don't!' Tina saw Bubbles' bewildered look and softened her tone. 'You'd better come in and explain yourself.' She offered him a seat in the kitchen. 'I hope you like sausage rolls in the middle of the night.'

He did. And jelly. And blancmange. In fact he had a curiously pleasing appetite for monosodium glutamate and a full range of foods containing E numbers. Tina watched with satisfaction as he ridded the kitchen of unwanted food and told his story.

'So, Rhona thinks you're Wig from this group When?'

''Fraid so.'

'Well *that* makes sense now. So you lied to her.'

'I didn't have to. They started feeding me, I swear. Her and that other kid. I can't play the guitar to save my life.'

He had tried, he assured her, but he couldn't master the chords on account of his fingernails overlapping the tips of his fingers. It had a name, and he tried to remember it with his cheeks full of pizza. Tina looked at his long black hair and lean face, and could see how Rhona might have mistaken him for Wig. He was no oil painting right now, though, and no mistake. His jaw was bristling with dark stubble, you could see blackheads on the side of his nose and his fingernails were dark with grime. His arms were white and flaccid and his clothes smelt of sweat and creosote. Even so, he had long eyelashes and a pleasing irregularity to his teeth. With a good clean-up he could look quite something.

He was twenty-four, he told them. He had deserted a university course in horticulture because his parents pushed him too hard. There were mammoth problems at home and he just couldn't live there, man. He wanted to go back to nature and find himself. Tina said he had better start looking quick or he could end up like her dead husband.

'Tell me about him.'

'Oh . . .' (He liked steamed vegetables and DIY and women with no lipstick. Apparently she stifled him.) ' . . . another time, perhaps.'

She said he could stay on the floor if he wanted, and then remembered that there wasn't one, apart from the one in the kitchen. He could have a bath and sleep in the spare room if he didn't mind balloons. She left him with Bubbles to sort out some clothes for him, and went up to bed. In the morning he would have to go. She already had two people to support.

Rhona had rejected all attempts at consolation and cried herself to sleep. At four in the morning she awoke to find Tina leaning over her, stroking her face.

'You cried out in your sleep.'

'No one came to my party,' she murmured.

'I'm sorry. It's early days, yet, pet. I'm so, so sorry . . .'

She asked Tina if she would sleep with her, and she curled up, foetus-like, cupped in the curve of Tina's body. She felt suddenly safe again. It was important to be felt sorry for. But she didn't tell Tina what she was really thinking at that moment. As she drifted off to sleep in the warmth of Tina's soft flesh, she felt relieved, in a way, that no one had turned up. If eleven-year-olds had gone home with balloon bears she would have been a laughing stock for weeks. Poor Tina: she did try.

The following day Tina went into town after work at three thirty. The post office queue snaked right across the room and back on account of some cord barriers which guided people in a zig-zag progression. Tina stood in a corner consulting a fat Yellow Pages volume and scribbling guiltily on the back of an envelope. She guarded the page with her left hand, in case anyone should see that it was headed 'Dating Agencies'.

As she looked up to scrutinise her uninterested audience, it occurred to her that there would be a Gabriel–Rhona confrontation in about an hour, and some disillusion would follow. She decided not to rush home and warn Rhona. She didn't want to be the bearer of any more bad news, and had a feeling that, this time, the messenger might be shot. She would stay out shopping and enjoy her afternoon off.

Was she selfish? Was she neglecting a duty in failing to provide Rhona with a father? It was far too soon to think about new husbands. She bought a local paper and sat reading the 'Two's Company' section in the small ads. She stared at the form to fill in ('not more than twenty-five words') and wondered what she would put *if*, just if, she were obliged to fill one in, let's say.

It had to be said that she still wanted a child, but the child she still wanted was Cameron's. If only she could get used to the idea that another man could father an equally lovely baby. Cameron, after all, was not going to come back. But it would take years to get to know a stranger well enough to want his child, and then maybe it would be too late.

Cameron had told her she was obsessed. She was impatient; if she loved him she would wait. So she sweated it out over beans on toast and cleaned ketchup off tables while he examined microfiches in cool student libraries, drank cappuccinos and built up his sperm supply. And then one day he said it (how could she have forgotten such cruelty?) once when he was being neurotic over some illness of Rhona's: 'If you were a mother you'd understand.' *If you were a mother*. It just slipped out. Hadn't she mothered his daughter for years? Hadn't she longed for motherhood herself? He apologised later, of course. But he had still said it, cordoned himself off by a rite of passage: parenthood. The real McCoy.

She was in frozen foods when she found herself magnetically drawn to the clothes section of the department store, and in particular to one area of it: a corner called 'Babywear'. She scanned the rails of '12–18 months' and '6–12 months' and came to '0–3 months' and 'New Born'. She fondled miniature bodysuits and vests, held out cardigans small enough for dolls, and smiled as she do-se-doed through 'Booties and Mitts'. A film of tears put everything out of focus. The sleepsuits hung up like little people with short flat legs. She said, 'Ah, sod it!' and bought a '0–3 months' bear-print sleepsuit and a pair of the smallest red wellington boots.

'Boy or girl?' asked the cashier, jauntily.

Tina hesitated, then looked down and tapped her empty belly. 'Don't know yet.'

'Ah! Stocking up, are we? That's half the fun, isn't it?' She handed her the change, 'Oh, you'll love it!'

On the bus she kept peeking at the label: '0–3 months'. Such a bold and awe-inspiring statement. What a thing to be nought! Nought months, nought days, nought anything. Just a little round zero, breathing and bewildered, bundled into a dolly's suit and precious beyond compare. The boots were for toddlers, but they conjured up little feet so instantly you could touch them. She held them inside the bag, pointing the toes together and then apart, fondling the red plastic exactly as she would when there were feet inside them.

When she returned home Gabriel was wandering around the house with a bare torso and eating toast. Bubbles was ironing his jeans and singing, 'Now, ah'm the king of the swingers (yeah!), the jungle VIP . . .' to herself. He'd had a good ten hours to get dressed, thought Tina, you'd think he could've managed to put a shirt on.

Rhona called from the top of the stairs, 'Wig! *Wig!* Come up and see me in my dress!'

'Wig?' frowned Tina. 'You haven't told her, have you?'

He stuffed the remainder of the toast into his mouth, turned the kettle on and shrugged.

'Not yet.'

Not yet? How long was he planning on staying?

'She can't cope with being lied to right now,' she said.

'Exactly! Why spoil things for her? She's getting a big kick out of it. And you've gained a few Brownie points letting me stay here, I can tell you.'

Tina watched as he inspected the teapot, and noticed that he was wearing a pair of Cameron's corduroy trousers.

'And who do *I* think you are? Am I supposed to be in on your stardom, or do I think you're Gabriel who's trying to find the meaning of life in people's garden sheds?'

'Plain old Gabe.' He made himself comfortable in a chair and hugged one knee. 'Hey, I tried to wash my clothes earlier. You wanna get a new washing machine.'

Hmm.

'You're dead right. I do want to get a new washing machine.'

Who did he think he was, coming in off the streets and complaining about her electrical equipment?

'Nice teapot, though,' he conceded.

'Spout's all up the creek,' she said, coming over all Mr Pooley-ish suddenly.

She would let him stay for one cup of tea, and then he would have to go. And he would have to tell Rhona the truth, otherwise she would be cast in the role of killjoy again. And anyway, life was getting too complicated. She was supposed to think he was Gabe, Rhona thought he was Wig and Bubbles – off and on – thought he was Cameron. *He* was still trying to find out who the hell he was, whilst depleting her Persil Automatic into the bargain. It just wasn't on.

'I want you to know,' she said as he made to follow Rhona's squeals up the stairs, 'that you won't find the meaning of life in our kitchen. We can't afford it.'

He patted her arm. 'No worries,' he said.

She looked at her arm in amazement.

'Shoo-bee-doo! I wanna be like yoo-hoo-hoo!' sang Bubbles.

Was she mad? No one wanted to be like Tina.

Vanilla

Three days after the party Gabriel was still there. He had spotted a niche in the Morrisons' domestic life and homed in on it with dogged determination before his shirt was dry enough to wear. He offered to do some work on the house in exchange for basic accommodation for a while; he could do plastering and painting and his carpentry skills stretched as far as floorboards. But Tina said she wanted to do it all herself, and surprised herself by meaning it. When he offered to convert the garden into anything she wanted she was tempted, but when he offered to take daily care of Bubbles into the bargain, she gave in. Just for a few weeks.

With the changed routine came a new concept of time. Sometimes it proceeded sluggishly like a watched clock, the second hand shuffling from one notch to the next with the minute hand following in a frustrating dawdle. But at other times – more often now – it seemed to race ahead so quickly it was impossible to complete anything but the essentials in waking hours. You got up, prepared breakfast, washed up, and before you knew it there were only a few moments before midday. And then if anyone waylaid you, chatted to you or led you astray with a cup of tea – or if some unforeseen incident occurred – it was teatime before you could say 'Bob's your uncle'. A phone call or two and a daydream and it was time for bed. A few more chores, another load of washing and a bath and it was way past bedtime. And nothing exceptional had been accomplished. It was as though the day had been shortened permanently by some new legislation, but with minutes that could chug on for ever.

Since Cameron died there had been a lot of empty time; hours that dragged and hours that were completely unaccounted for. Working on the house was a kind of therapy, a way of seeing some progress in the days and weeks that passed relentlessly, yielding so little. Sometimes Tina wondered too if it was a way of identifying with him, becoming closer to him by stepping into his shoes and completing his activities for him. Other times she felt she might be consoling Rhona by behaving like Cameron, or, unconsciously, trying to be loved like him.

At times she thought she felt his presence. The smell of his shoes in the corner by the wardrobe, an unfinished letter in the bureau, a magazine turned face down at the page he had been reading ('Eliminate free radicals and live longer'), shirts she'd left unwashed in the laundry bin: any of these could conjure him up on the spot, a real reading, writing, smelling person. But he never stayed, and she was left with a sharp aching in the walls of her stomach. She yearned to turn the clocks back and say one last thing, hold him close just one last time, have a warmer, more dignified farewell. The days slipped by with their sharp beginnings and ends, but there seemed no end to sadness and longing.

One day she saw Cameron standing at the foot of the garden. He wore green corduroys and an old felt hat he used for gardening. He was raking at a border, and his movements – free and chaotic – left her with a sharp ache of recognition. The tips of her fingers trembled like whiskers.

She approached slowly, reverently. 'Cameron!' she whispered.

He turned. Perhaps it was half a second – maybe less – before she saw, under the crumpled ruin of the hat, Gabriel's startled eyes.

Silence.

The air was warm and mellow with breeze, and smelt of freshly turned earth.

'I'm sorry. I thought . . . for a moment I thought—'

'*I'm* sorry. The clothes – Bubbles said it was OK. I should've . . . I'm sorry.'

'No, no – it's fine,' she said quickly to disguise disappointment, which came crashing in on her and seemed to be pressing at her skull. 'It's a good idea.'

* * *

Gabriel proved an impressive worker. Bubbles was hardly ever out of his sight, happily supervising him from the sidelines as he turned part of the vegetable patch into a herb garden. Tina sold the car – a rusty grey Ford with three weeks' tax and MOT – for two hundred and fifty pounds, and bought equipment for the house at special rates from work; she gave Gabriel what remained to buy things for the garden. He mowed the lawn, trimmed the edges of all the borders and planted alyssum, lobelia and primroses. Behind these he retrained galloping clematis and honeysuckle up trellises and pruned the clambering roses. He dug up the vegetable garden, turning the soil and planting out lettuces, runner beans and carrots. He set up bamboo canes and tended seedlings in rows of neat boxes. He marked spots of earth with wooden tags: 'Mint', 'Thyme', 'Parsley', 'Basil'. He weeded round the rampant budding lavender, coaxed clouds of Baby's Breath up support canes, cut back the brambles clawing over the porch, and cleaned out the tool shed. In one corner of the garden he stacked bricks into a square to house a compost heap, and beside it he filled binliners with leaky watering cans, rusty trowels and broken shards of terracotta. At the edge of the garden he repaired a gash in a crumbling Cotswold stone wall, carefully replacing the upstanding stones and going on long walks in the hills to find a replica of one last piece of stone which had shattered into clean yellow fragments.

Tina watched him carefully, awaiting his departure with the completion of the garden, certain his role as granny-minder would dwindle fast. But he seemed genuinely tender towards Bubbles. He spent hours in her company, listening to her stories and drawing her out on old embroidered memories. She started to dress more smartly too, taking greater care with detail and abandoning her perm for good. Each day he took her on a long walk and she came home with bright cheeks and rioting hair. One day she returned with flame red hair, strands of coloured thread woven into two tiny plaits each side of her face. Tina laughed at first, then realised her mistake with a look from Gabriel. Bubbles was vibrant. She still bought ham, but she put herb bouquets in pots and planted seeds in egg boxes. Her zip-up bag was often open with the heads of flowers poking out, or the tips of potted plants.

Tina thought she had misjudged him. She had thought him arrogant, but he seemed kind. He did have his faults; he ate toast to an extent which compared only to one other person: Cameron. She bristled every time she saw the crumbs. There were crumbs on the table, on the chairs and in the plughole. The floor crunched underfoot with toast crumbs, every plate in the sink had crumbs stuck to it with jam, and there were collages of crumbs on every worktop. The grill resembled the sawdusted floor of a hamster cage. He would wander around the house with great doorsteps of toast in hand; he collected the post with toast in his mouth; he washed up (occasionally) eating toast; and he talked on the phone in his thick crumb-coated socks between mouthfuls of toast. Perhaps it was a young man's nerves that had made him overplay the confidence bit. At any rate, she trusted him and grew to like his presence and even his relentless advice.

'What's your secret?' she asked one evening in the kitchen.

He looked defensive. 'I've got no secrets.'

'Come on. I mean, how do you do it? You've *transformed* Bubbles. You always seem so . . . so happy to be here.'

'I am.'

'Why? I know nothing about you. I've been so wound up with myself. I want to know everything. Tell me.'

He frowned and looked at her intently for a while, as if he had something important to say. 'I've been meaning to tell you . . .' He went to turn the light switch on, but hesitated and opened a drawer instead. He placed a squat vanilla-scented candle on the kitchen table and lit it. 'You've got a crate of wine out the back – how about we break open a bottle? You deserve a drink.'

She got up to fetch one, but he motioned her to stay. 'Here's one I brought in earlier,' he said, already uncorking it.

She smiled with one half of her face and sank back into her chair. She watched him in the candlelight, pouring the wine, taking control. He came towards her and set the glass beaker on the table. Then he knelt down and started to tug at her boots. It was all a bit clumsy in the end; one sock came off and he hit his head on the corner of the table. But he retrieved supremacy in the situation and replaced the sock gently, laying both her feet on a low stool.

'Now,' he said, resuming his position at the end of the table, 'what's *your* secret?'

She thought he was going to congratulate her on coping so well in difficult circumstances, and she breathed a faint laugh. But the question still seemed to be there, and he was looking straight at her.

'I think you're the one with a secret, Tina.'

'Me? With *my* life? In *this* house? No chance. What you see is what you get. Plain old reliable old Tina.'

But he kept looking at her. 'Everyone has a story that isn't told, a story no one knows of. What's yours?'

She stared at the tall triangle of flame between them and blotted out his face. She said nothing. A strong smell of vanilla filled the air. Eventually she took in a sharp breath and picked up her glass. Then she wriggled her toes and looked back at the lengthening flame.

'You don't say much about yourself, do you?' he said. 'I mean, you've just lost a husband and you haven't even grieved or anything.'

She refocused quickly, catching the dark velvety eyes unawares. 'How the hell do *you* know I haven't grieved? How can you say what I have or haven't done? I have to think about Rhona! I have to be . . . stable for her and everything. I can't just blubber all round the place!' She ran her hand through her woolly fringe. 'What would *you* know?'

It was hard to tell in the dim glow whether his eyes were wet or just sparkling, but she softened suddenly. 'Sorry! Sorry, sorry. I shouldn't have said that. Perhaps you've lost someone too.'

'Yes,' he said at last. They clearly were tears in his eyes. 'I have. I only wanted to help.'

'What *helps*?'

'Talking about it?'

'It?'

'Him. What was he like?'

'What do you mean, what was he like?'

'Well, was he a good bloke, this Cameron?'

She sat forward and flipped her fingers through the flame, thinking. 'He was . . . the best.'

'Kind?' asked Gabriel, helpfully.

'Yeah. That.'

'Generous?'

'I reckon so.'

'Would you say he was handsome?'

'I suppose. Sometimes. Who cares?'

'I want to know.'

'*Why?*'

'I'm just trying . . . look, OK, kind. How was he kind?'

'Well, he was a great father to Rhona. He would do anything for her. He spent hours singing her to sleep when she was little.'

'What about you?'

'Oh, you know. Everything. He used to do all the decorating. He was doing up this house for us.'

'For all of you.'

'OK. That was for us. But he used to do things for me. You know, like you just then. He'd massage my feet, make me cocoa. He never went out with the lads or nothing. We had to save hard, but he always spent the money on *us.*'

'So he worked, then?'

'Well, the last couple of years – as a trainee solicitor – but he was about to earn a lot.'

'So he was clever.'

'Oh, yes. He was *very* clever. I never met anyone cleverer. Not ever. He could use words like . . . you know . . . he could put words together in a way which was magic. Oh, and he had a conscience too. He hated cruelty to animals. We weren't allowed to wear leather or eat meat.' She smiled. 'He was fanatical sometimes.'

'Not neurotic, though?'

'Oh no. Nothing like that. Though sometimes . . .'

She remembered that Cameron was unable to wear turtle-necked sweaters because every time he put the neck over his head he had a re-birthing experience. Was that neurotic or what? She had unwittingly bought one for his birthday in the first year of their marriage. It had cost her an arm and a leg, but he only wore it a few times (all difficult deliveries) and then he sneakily gave it to Oxfam. The following year she bought him a cardigan. He could have as many Caesarian sections as he liked.

' . . . well, not especially.'

'And Rhona's not yours, is she?'

'She is now. She knows no other mother.'

'Yeah, I know. I mean, did he have any other children?'

He sounded like a reporter now, hungry for information. 'Any with you, for example?'

She stamped the palm of her hand down on the candle and the flame went out. 'Ouch!' A strong carbony smoke filled the air and they sat in darkness. The washing machine light flashed a red 'Completed'. Outside a moth hit the window pane and flew away.

When he turned the light on there were tear paths glistening on her cheeks and she was wiping her face. He put his arms round her and she wept. They stood for five minutes, rocking gently. She buried her cheek in his shoulder and gulped him in. He smelt just like Cameron.

'Do you think I need a man?' she asked at last, blotting her eyes.

He went to take out the load from the washing machine and examined a cardigan of Bubbles'. 'What you need is comfort.'

'I can't afford fabric softener.'

Gabe shook his head and folded some clothes. 'Do *you* think you need a man?'

'Rhona does.'

'And you?'

'I don't feel very loved sometimes. I miss it. I miss being loved . . . as a woman.'

He fitted the woollens on to hangers. 'Why don't you read some old love letters?'

She explained that Cameron hadn't written love letters. He hadn't needed to. Theirs wasn't the sort of relationship that relied on sentiment. He may have been penniless, but he respected her, loved her. Theirs was a love built on loyalty, trust, humour, deep passion. They hadn't needed mushy love tokens.

Not one sodding love letter.

Thyme Green

It was the last Sunday in May. The sky was overcast, and rain fell in a steady drizzle. It dripped from the leafy trees and ran down the roof, spilling over the clogged guttering. It ran down the walls, collecting in every crack and stone hollow. It dribbled down the window panes and seeped in behind the putty. It ran down the chimney breasts and leaked in behind the broken flashings, oozed along the rafters, swelling the wood, dripping on to the plasterboard ceilings in pools of grey and brown. It ran inside the chimney stacks, mixing with soot into a jet dye which penetrated the brickwork in places and stained the plaster. There was a dank, dispiriting smell throughout the house.

Tina was chipping away at crumbling plaster in the dining room, a dark, north-facing room, which seemed gloomier still in the rain. She used a cold chisel and a club hammer and had already exposed patches of yellow stone mapped in the sea of white. She could hear clunking sounds coming from the annexe as if furniture were being moved around, and Bubbles singing loudly:

> 'Come all you fair and tender maids
> That flourish in your prime, prime,
> Beware, beware, keep your gardens fair,
> And let no man steal your thyme, thyme,
> And let no man steal your thyme.
>
> For when your thyme is passed and gone
> He'll care no more for you, you,

And every place that your thyme would waste
Will all spread o'er with rue, rue
Will all spread o'er with rue . . .'

When they spent the first weekend together, Cameron had cleaned her teeth for her. She remembered how gently he had stroked the brush inside her mouth and made her rinse, tilting the cup tentatively, patting with a towel a dribble of water that spilled over the corners of her mouth.

She recalled also how irritated she used to be by his own toothbrushing. He started off well enough. The front teeth were cleaned without any ado, but before long the strokes on the back teeth built up into a sort of frenzy, like the noise of an old steam train starting up. It seemed to her that he kept the brush still and moved his head up and down. And he did something strange with his mouth to make a hollow sawing sound which filled the whole bathroom and echoed down the landing. And these things got buried along with coffins if you weren't careful. It was all too easy to reduce your whole life together to one tiny package, to chop off all the toothbrushings and skirmishes and be left with one neat little bundle of sunny days, smiley breakfasts like cornflake advertisements and candlelit meals. And there was another case in point. Despite all his fanaticism about healthy eating, Cameron always finished a meal out with chocolate fudge cake. He wouldn't entertain trying a pub restaurant that didn't offer high doses of chocolate to finish with. And then he would always get some around his mouth. Just a little, but enough to make him look like a child in a high chair. Some days she hated him for his lack of competence at handling a spoon, other days she loved the vulnerability of that look as he paid self-importantly with a credit card, oblivious of his chocky mouth. And then there was the kiss which smelt of chocolate. No use telling him to clean his teeth.

Now Tina longed for him to be here anyway, brushing away in the bathroom or snorting down some chocolate dessert or other. She would dance to the beat of his dental hygiene, lovingly lick off his chocolate fudge. How petty our sensibilities, she thought, when life spoils us with normality.

The head of the club hammer was wobbling dangerously, and she decided to stop using it. Their only other good hammer was under the bed, where it had been since Cameron's death. She would never have been able to use it on an intruder (she couldn't even picture bringing it down on someone's poor head) but its presence there had consoled her in the angry darkness. She went to the bedroom now and knelt down to retrieve the hammer. As she reached under the bed her hand brushed the corner of a piece of card parked under the centre of the bedframe. She stretched to pull it out, and examined it solemnly. It was the back of a cornflake packet, and on the blank side were ruled lines with dates and figures crammed in between in various changes of biro ink: *Fri 37°20, Sat 37°06, Sun 37°39, Mon 36°76!!!* Tuesday was almost entirely obliterated by giant capitals proclaiming *OVULATION! Today's the day!!*

'Today's the day . . .' said Tina wearily. Tuesday was the day she had been waiting for. The slight drop in temperature on Monday signalled the most fertile day on Tuesday, and that day, above all others, they would try for the most longed-for child in the universe. Tuesday was also the day Cameron died.

She returned to the dining room and thumped the wall. A clump of plaster fell out of it. Breathing very deeply, she stood back to see if there was any more to do, and noticed some cracks on the wall next to the walk-in cupboard. She started chipping, and this time there was a hollow, clunking sound. She tapped a bit more, and the chisel sank completely into the wall. As she pulled it out, there was a loud cracking sound, and splinters of wood appeared around the hole. She took the hammer and belted it against the surface. A whole sheet of plaster slipped off to the floor, and a great gash gaped in the wall, exposing what appeared to be a small lift. When the dust had settled, she pulled back shards of wood and saw a rope pulley inside. Hesitantly, she tugged at the rope, and the pulley began to move, until a wooden tray appeared. There, hidden between the two inner walls and above the old cellar, was a dumb waiter.

She sat on a stepladder and stared at the gashed wall for some time: at what she had done and what she had uncovered, making connections. She saw more and more of herself in the house, and shuddered at its cruelly appropriate gesture. Tina Morrison: dumb waiter.

. . . Beware, beware, keep your gardens fair,
And let no man steal your thyme, thyme,
And let no man steal your thyme.

Her nostrils twitched, and she went to fetch the vacuum cleaner.

On Tuesday morning Rhona said of her grandmother, 'She *smells.*' Bubbles poured some cereal shakily, and Tina flinched on her behalf. She could never be sure that Bubbles had felt the full force of Rhona's bluntness, but the statement was stingingly true, and she felt it was her responsibility to deal with things.

After breakfast she inspected the bathroom cabinet. Bubbles seemed to possess only an old aerosol deodorant which was years old and gave out a small dribble of fizzing liquid when pressed. Tina sniffed it. It could have been insect repellent. She searched through the bottles on the window ledge and a drawer in her own bedroom, and found a classy deodorant stick she had never opened. It had been one of Cameron's early presents: a perfume she didn't use. She caught hold of Bubbles' sleeve as she made her way to her annexe.

'Here – use this,' she whispered.

'What is it?' asked Bubbles, whispering back.

'It's to make you smell nice.'

'Oh. Right-ee-o.'

Tina sank into a heavy velvet sofa later that morning and looked about her. She was in a poky room decorated with pink paint and leafy plants. In front of her a woman with frosted lipstick the same colour as the walls was leafing through a desk diary and smiling. She came to sit next to Tina on the sofa.

'Gerald will be through in a moment with some coffee,' she said brightly. 'Now, Christina, let's start with what we offer, and then you can tell me a little about yourself.'

Tina listened numbly as the pink woman explained how she and Gerald would make a short video of her, how she could see it herself, and how she had absolutely free access to the videos of up to three men per week, and all for only one hundred and ninety-five pounds.

Tina was gathering her shopping bags, saying she had made a mistake, when Gerald came in bearing a tray of coffee and biscuits. 'Now sit yourself back down, Chrissy,' he said. 'We've got something *you* want, and *we're* short on women at the moment. I'm sure we can do a deal.'

The woman looked startled and then smiled, waiting to take her cue from Gerald.

'We'll make the video absolutely free, and you pay us the full fee only if you find a partner!'

'Well . . .'

'Now come on, Christina. What price can you put on a partner for life?'

Tina smiled woodenly. She supposed it was a fair deal.

'Just relax and answer my questions as naturally as you can. No, don't look at the camera. Oh dear! We can't see your face. Could you just push your hair back – right back – that's fine. Nice bright smile – *smile* – just act natural. Action, Gerald! Now, Christina, you're about five foot four, I believe?'

'Five foot six.'

'I see. Now, Chris, what sort of food do you like?'

'Um . . .'

'When you go out for a meal, where do you like to go? French? Italian? Indian?'

'Oh, anything really. I don't go out that much.'

'So you're a woman of wide tastes. I see. Now, Chrissy, tell us a bit about your hobbies.'

'I . . . I . . .'

'What sort of sports do you enjoy?'

'None really. I don't enjoy sport.'

'You like walking, though?'

'Yes. Yes, I like walking.'

'And other hobbies?'

Tina was silent. She felt she was letting this woman down and desperately wanted to say the right thing. She swallowed and opened her mouth to speak, but nothing came out.

'What sort of films do you like?'

'Anything, really – well, romantic, I suppose. And comedy.'

'Romantic and comedy. So you don't like the sort of man who watches action movies?'

'Oh no. I don't mind, really. My husband – my late husband – used to watch blood and guts boys' own stuff – it didn't bother me. I mean, I just left him to it.'

'Right. And what else do you do in your spare time?'

'I don't really have spare time.'

'You're in sales, I believe.'

'Sales? Oh, yes!'

'You must be very high-powered to have no spare time at all.'

'Oh, no. But I have this big house. I'm doing it up in my spare time. I spend about three days a week on it.'

'So would you say you were a fanatic about DIY?'

'N—'

'Excellent! So you're mad about DIY, Christina, and you have very broad tastes in food and entertainment and a passion for walking. You're really a very home-loving type, aren't you? What sign of the zodiac are you?'

Tina looked at Gerald for support, but Gerald simply waved his hand to focus her back to Julia.

'Taurus.'

'And are you a typical Taurean, would you say, Chris?'

'I'm not sure.'

'Practical, reliable, difficult to get to know but loyal and affectionate?'

'I'd like to think—'

'And what qualities are you looking for in a partner?'

'Um—' But Julia was going to help her out.

'Are you looking for a man who is loving, reliable and generous?'

'I—'

'Someone who can wine and dine you – because you *do* like your meals out, don't you? – but he doesn't have to be fit—'

'Oh, I think I'd prefer fit.' She was getting the hang of this now.'

'But you're not the sporty type yourself. Someone with a good sense of humour who could share your passion for DIY. Well, thank you, Christina, for sharing your thoughts with us, and—'

'Kind, I think.'

'I beg your pardon?'

'Kind. I'd like a kind partner.'

'Cut! Gerald, cut!'

Gerald emerged from behind the camera and smiled. 'Jolly well done, Chrissy.'

'I think we might just need to run through that again, Gerald. It's probably best not to mention previous partners, Christina. Men like to think they're unique. They don't like to think of you as second-hand. I mean, I know you *are*, but we have to keep up their illusions, don't we?'

Tina was pink-cheeked and perspiring with nerves. Gerald managed to edit the video without a second sitting, and after two more coffees he played it back. It was only about three minutes long. Tina watched herself mumbling through a mound of hair in a monotone voice.

Her reward was ten minutes alone with a file of male mug-shots. She choked as she turned the pages of lonely people, each one longing enough for love to lay themselves bare in three paragraphs of trivial personal details. She wondered if Ron the bald solicitor or Mike the divorced engineer had divulged the secrets of their zodiac signs without protest. She chose a lab technician called Andy. They would write if Andy liked her video too.

When Tina slipped home at noon to tackle the living room, she saw from a hundred yards away a flashing blue light as she rounded a bend in the road. She started to walk faster, and broke into a run when she realised it was outside number twenty-three.

Inside, a stretcher was being hoisted off the floor and she saw Bubbles' surprised face peeking out above the blanket.

'What is it?' she panted.

'Are you a friend?' asked a woman paramedic.

'Family. She's my—' she had meant to say 'mother-in-law', but it came out as 'responsibility'.

The woman ushered Tina into the bedroom, and produced an object in a polythene bag. 'Does she usually use this?' She pointed to the deodorant stick.

'Well, no. I gave it to her this morning.' Tina frowned, and added, 'It is *safe*, isn't it?'

'Oh yes. In the right hands.' She pointed through the polythene at an instruction around the base of the wide, flattish tube: 'PUSH UP BOTTOM'.

Tina groaned and sank on to the bed. She collapsed dramatically, throwing her feet into the air and flopping her hands by her sides.

'Nothing serious, but there've been some complications,' said the bemused ambulance woman. 'There'll be a bit of ulceration, and she'll need a stitch or two.'

Pacific Blue

Tina sat cross-legged in the cellar, poring over a fat DIY book. It was late afternoon and hot outside, but the cellar was damp and musty. It seemed a difficult, useless room and she wished it weren't there at all. 'Cellar.' She traced the words with her finger, muttering. She had to treat the walls with a bituminous waterproofing compound or – better still – a moisture-curing polymer. The urethane resin in this liquid would set by the action of moisture upon it and form a water-resistant film. If that didn't work, she'd have to remove all the plaster and line the walls with waterproof lining material, then replaster. She wrote a list.

'Hey, Tina!' came a familiar voice down the cellar steps. 'You're spending too much time in the cellar. You wanna start with the roof, look. That's where it's all happening. You can't do anything 'ness you get your roof sorted first.'

She clambered to her feet and went up the gritty steps to where Keith Pooley stood smiling. He followed her to the kitchen and she filled the kettle.

'Rhona let me in,' he said, nodding at Rhona who was seated at the table, designing something with crayons. 'I've brought you a slate ripper to replace the broken tiles – I'll show you how he works in a minute – and also a ladder. I noticed that ladder you been using is too short and he hasn't got a stand-off. You must always have *at least* three rungs extending beyond a roof's edge to get yourself up on to a roof, and you must always lean it against a solid surface.'

'Oh.'

'Now, you got it leaning up against the guttering. That's dangerous. So I've brought you my one with a stand-off – that's an aluminium stay which juts out and rests against the wall underneath or whatever.'

'Oh, well. Thank you.'

'And really you should have someone at the bottom of the ladder to steady it. I'd be quite happy—'

'I'm going to be doing it all on my own,' she said, placing the teapot on the table-mat in front of Rhona. 'Have a seat.'

He pulled a chair out adjacent to Rhona's. 'Oh, yes, of course. Well, in that case, make sure the bottom of the ladder is secure by tying it to a fixed object – like stakes in the ground, for example. But tie it by the stiles, not the rungs, and at about the height of the fifth rung. Here, I got you this leaflet on ladder safety from the store.'

'Mr Pooley brought us some honey,' said Rhona, not looking up from her drawing. 'Do you keep bees, then?'

'Well, I look after them for old Mrs Burton in that big house over by Buttercup Lane.'

'How do bees make honey?'

'Well, it's the workers who make the honey. They have a tough old life, the workers. They start working as soon as they've got the strength to stand, and they toil until their death, which – in the summer – is only about six weeks. They've got a mother but no children, no play, no fun, no nothing. Just work. The queen, now, she just sits there and lays over three thousand eggs a day!'

Tina felt like a worker. She poured the tea, deeply envious of the queen.

'Why do they hum, then,' Rhona continued, 'if they're not happy?'

'Ah, well. The bee's humming is made by the movement of its wings. If it waves them too slow, like, then you hear nothing. Nor if it waves them too fast. There's lots of sounds we can't hear, just like – for example – there's lots of colours we can't see. And other things. But if the vibrations made by the bee's wings are at just the right rate, and if it's near enough, then we can hear the humming.'

Tina was calculating the time, and hoped he wouldn't stay too long. She leafed through the pamphlet on ladders.

'What's that you're drawing, Rhona?' he asked, looking at her complicated geometrical image. Rhona was designing a fitted piano. She explained how it went all the way round the living room, like a fitted carpet, and you could sit down at it at any point and play. You could also, at the touch of a button, change the sound to any instrument you fancied.

'That's amazing!' said Keith, craning his neck to admire the design.

'Only trouble is,' sighed Rhona, 'I can't work out how to do the corners.'

'Ah! You've got a problem with the chimney breast and the alcoves too. Let's see, you've got a good mitre join there.'

'Mmm. But what do I do with the keys? I thought maybe they could get smaller and smaller here . . . and one big wedge-shaped one here.'

'Or a wooden wedge with a flowerpot on it, perhaps.'

'Yes! But then I was going to have just one middle C, with the notes getting lower and lower one way, and higher and higher the other. Then I could put a flowerpot where they joined.'

'Well, if you had more middle Cs you could have more people playing it. You could just have different sounds – you know – you could have a harpsichord keyboard, a clavinova, a synthesizer – a Roland E series or a Korg – and a pipe organ, maybe. You could sit down anywhere, like, and just start playing.'

'That's true. But how would you know where they began and ended? I want an unbroken keyboard.'

'Hmm. Some sort of pictures on the wall? Or the wedges in the alcoves? What about the radiator? You gonna get rid of that?'

'Oh, no. That could be the winter area, to keep your knees warm.'

'Got you!'

Tina wished she wouldn't encourage him, else he'd never go. But he got up of his own accord when Gabriel came in. They just stood and stared at each other.

Keith Pooley was staggered. Tina had told him she had no sons – did she really not know? Who did she think he was, then, this young man staying in her house? Why had she let him in? Or was she genuinely unaware he was her husband's love child? It seemed so obvious to Keith. But that look – those eyes – betrayed intrigue or panic, for certain. People said Mr Morrison had fallen off a ladder (Brenda from Garden Furniture had told him) but he wasn't so sure. He couldn't help knowing everything that happened in Moorhampton, but he knew how to mind his own business, and that was what he would do.

'This is Gabriel,' said Tina. 'He's . . . babysitting. I'm going out later.'

'Oh, well then. I'll be off. I've got a few things to do myself before I go out.' And he was gone.

'There's a gentleman here for you!' Bubbles shouted up the stairs.

'Help! Show him into the kitchen, will you?'

'I already have.'

When Tina came downstairs she could hear the man's gentle voice posing the remains of a long question to Bubbles: ' . . . so do you have any strong feelings about French nuclear testing in the South Pacific?'

She thought she had better save Bubbles from certain humiliation, but to her surprise Bubbles seemed to be having one of her lucid days.

'I think it's dreadful. We only have one planet, and we should protect it.'

'That's right—'

'I'm in contact with others, myself, of course—'

'You are? Tell me about that.'

'I used to be a mystic. It's been some time now since I had a contact, but you never lose the skill, you know. People are so *arrogant* to think earth has the monopoly of intelligent life—'

Tina burst into the kitchen breathlessly, sticking a grip into her hair. 'I'm sorry I've kept you.'

She stood against a cabinet to take in her date who was sitting at the table. He had short blond hair and a dark suit, smarter than she remembered him in the video. He sat with a very straight back and his spidery hands fumbled with the pepper pot.

'Have you come far?' asked Tina.

'Bristol – not too far.'

Tina hadn't banked on people from out of town applying to the agency, and hoped he didn't expect her to move to his area.

'Well, would you like a drink?'

'No thank you – I don't.'

'Ah! Tea?'

'No thank you. Your mother already asked me.' He smiled. 'I was asking her what she thought about the French nuclear testing in the South Pacific. Do you have any strong feelings about that?'

Tina thought for a moment.

'Some Enchanted Evening!' said Bubbles, on a roll.

'What?'

'Some Enchanted Evening. That was in *South Pacific.* And that other one . . . what was it?'

'Bubbles, why don't you go up the Co-op? I think we're running out of ham. They're open till eight tonight.'

Tina suddenly felt that she had lost the art of conversation, so she asked him for *his* opinions instead.

'Well,' he replied, 'I wonder what we've achieved in the fifty years since Nagasaki. I mean, have we really seen progress?'

Tina had the uncomfortable feeling that he was going to keep asking her difficult questions.

'Take TV,' he said, when she hesitated. 'I see you have a TV over there. It was still in its naive infancy in 1945 . . .' (*naive infancy*?) ' . . . today it's a condoned thief and interloper in almost every home of the developed world and every village of the developing world.'

Steady on.

Tina thought that now might be a good time to address the geographical problem.

'I hadn't expected anyone from Bristol.'

'We're just the same as anyone else,' he smiled.

She summoned up all her courage. 'No. I mean, I think you should know: I'm not prepared to move to another area.'

'Oh.' He looked perplexed for a moment. 'That's really no problem. God has no problems with space.'

'God? You *are* a good-humoured, non-smoking atheist, aren't you?'

'No. I'm a good-humoured, non-smoking Jehovah's Witness.'

Tina's jaw dropped open. 'Who let you in?' Even as she spoke her head was turning to Bubbles.

'Gotta Wash That Man Right Outa My Hair,' said Bubbles. 'That was the one!'

The doorbell rang. It was a good-humoured atheist.

* * *

Rhona told Gabriel it was her bath night, and called down to him from the bathroom for nearly half an hour, asking for her back to be scrubbed. Life still seemed like a curious dream: first her father dying in this strange house, and now Wig living under the very same roof, sharing their meals, using the same soap, breathing the same air. Just when she thought her heart had stopped fluttering each time she saw him, she would glimpse him sweeping back his jet black hair or hear him pronounce her name with that perfect accent that no one round their way used, and she would have to sit down to avoid falling down. She studied her old clippings about him religiously to check his likes and dislikes, and made sure she pandered to every little foible she could (his obsession with peanut butter, for example, and his love of liquorice and pickled onions and the colour mauve). She was sometimes a little disappointed at his lack of enthusiasm for her attentiveness, but she put it down to his obvious anxiety.

Gabriel did not respond now to her calling, and when she eventually emerged from the bathroom she scurried down the stairs, wrapped in a towel, to find and seduce her babysitter. The door of the dining room was ajar, and Gabriel sat on the bare wooden boards surrounded by photographs. She could see him hunched over an album, just a nose protruding from two drapes of hair. She approached softly, leaving little damp footprints behind her. He looked up, startled, and she saw that his face was wet with tears.

'Ah!' he said, wiping his cheeks with a sleeve. 'The little mermaid emerges at last.'

He snapped the album shut and stuffed the photographs into the shoebox where they were kept. Rhona was flummoxed. He was supposed to be shocked or thrilled, not tearful. She had toyed with the idea of dropping the towel and appearing naked before him, but her left nipple had started to grow before her right one, and she wasn't sure he'd be impressed. In any case, a hint of nakedness was just that little bit more alluring than the whole hog. She turned to give him the benefit of her flawless back, but she could hear him slamming the albums into a pile and saying, 'Come on! Get some clothes on quick, before you catch your death!'

She turned to look at him from the door. His eyes were red and puffy; hers were wide and filling with tears. She wiggled her toes and ran upstairs to change. He ran his hand through his hair and started to measure the skirting boards.

Andy bought Tina a drink in the lounge bar of the Lamb while she tried to take him in. She watched him standing at the bar; a well-covered man in his late forties with dull blond hair and a beige poplin raincoat. They sat and made small talk over two half-pints of stout, studying each other across the low pub table.

After half an hour Tina was shocked at how little they had in common. Not a film, not a hobby, not even a zodiac sign. They had been warned to keep this first meeting to an hour at most, so when he picked up his things to go, saying, 'Phew! Well, that went very well, don't you think?' and asked if she would like to see him again, she was only a little confused. How could she say no? Remember, it's a business relationship at this stage, Julia had said. Was it that easy? All the usual excuses didn't apply. Her very position as client at the dating agency made it abundantly clear that she, too, was desperately available. Nothing short of a dose of mumps could stop him from seeing her again.

When Rhona came back downstairs, after a sulk and a think, she found Bubbles and Gabriel putting the final piece of skirting board in place. The dining room looked like a real room at last. All it needed was a little plastering, some paint and a carpet.

'It's amazing!' said Rhona. 'And Bubbles, you've helped too. What have you done?'

'"I have married a house carpenter . . ."' sang Bubbles, piling the tools into an oily canvas bag. 'Isn't that your best dress you're wearing?'

Rhona gave a twirl. 'Do you like it, Gabe?'

Gabriel watched the twiglet legs attempt a fashionable strut across the room. The bones stuck out from the knees and she rocked slightly from side to side like a penguin. He felt a rush of love for this frail little person, so easily piqued.

'I'm going to hide! You two count to a hundred and then come looking for me!' She rushed off and hid in the broom cupboard, making sure to remove the key from the door first.

It didn't take Gabriel long to find her. She could hear him pretending to look everywhere else, long after he must've heard her cough from under the stairs. When he opened the door she hid behind some coats until he was fully inside. Then she slammed the door, leant against it and giggled.

'Got you!'

Gabriel could see nothing, but he smelt the musty odour of old raincoats and shoes and Rhona's fresh toothpasty breath inches from his nose. 'Rhona, stop messing around.'

'I'm not letting you go!' she squealed. She felt the key in her hot palm, placed it in the lock and turned it swiftly. 'See! I've locked us in! Now you're trapped here with me until I decide to let you go!'

'Rhona, come on. This is silly.'

'You'll have to kiss me first!'

'Rhona, give me the key!'

'You'll have to find it – it's somewhere on my body!' She was giggling hysterically now.

He caught hold of her hands and shouted roughly, 'Rhona!'

She stopped suddenly, and he couldn't see what change he had made to her face.

'I can't kiss you.'

'Why not?' She sounded limp and close to tears. He loathed himself for the tragedy he seemed to be causing in everyone's lives.

'You're too young.'

'I'm not. I'm eleven. You're twenty-four. What's wrong with that? When I'm twenty you'll be thirty-three. It's all right, Gabe. I've worked it out.'

'Look, I can't kiss you.'

There was a silence.

'You don't fancy me, do you?' It was a broken, plaintive voice, and Gabriel softened.

'It's not that. I can't kiss you because I . . . because I . . .' Rhona waited. 'I'm . . . not what you think.'

'Are you a homa sexule?'

He breathed a laugh. 'No. Look, come here.' He put his arms around her and squeezed tightly. Bubbles could be heard vacuuming in the living room. Then he suddenly began to tickle her. She dropped the key and he unlocked the door. They laughed and screamed and played until Tina came home at nine fifteen. But he felt very uneasy.

Terracotta

The following day Tina came home from work early to hear the television on in the dining room. It had been in the kitchen, covered with a sheet, for weeks. She crossed the hall and peeked round the door. Gabriel was sitting with his back to her, and facing her were images of Cameron, smiling into an amateur video camera. The shot homed in on a tiny baby which Tina lifted out of a Moses basket. They both marvelled at its feet and smiled some more at the camera, which veered off towards a waste-paper bin and back again. Then Gabriel rewound the tape and started to watch the scene again.

'What the hell are you doing?'

Gabriel turned a startled face to the door, and Tina marched over to the video player and pressed the stop button, surprising herself. She ejected the cassette and slammed it into its cardboard case.

'I was just—'

Nosing into other people's affairs, she wanted to say. 'These are *private* tapes!' How dare he rummage through her private tapes!

'I just got the video to work – I thought you'd be pleased. The tapes were all together . . .'

Tina was pacing around in a mood he had never witnessed. 'They *are* labelled! I suppose you just *happened* to pick up a private family tape instead of *Casablanca*, did you?'

'Hey, look! I'm sorry. What's the big deal? I'm really sorry. Calm down.'

'And who's done all this skirting board?'

'I did, last night.'

'Well I didn't ask you to. Just leave me to get on with my life *my* way.'

She ran into the kitchen and started slamming pots and pans around. He followed her, biting his lip. She continued throwing saucepans into the cupboard under the sink until she felt satisfied he knew how angry she was. Then she turned and spoke. 'What's going on? Rhona said you were crying over our photos. What are you doing in our house?'

'I told you. I just—'

'Why were you rewinding that tape? Tell me that!'

'I didn't realise you adopted Rhona so young. I got the impression she was older when you and Cameron got together. I was just curious, I guess.'

'She was two. Happy?' She grabbed the kettle and started to fill it, water catching on the lip and spraying the work surfaces.

'So who was the baby?'

She breathed heavily and waved a hand. 'Not Rhona. Just a baby – a boy.' The kettle overflowed and drenched her. 'I want you to leave.'

As he left to go to his room, Bubbles came in from the garden with her shopping bag and removed from it a Black & Decker power drill.

'What's that for?' asked Tina.

'I'm doing up my annexe.'

'Hmm. You should've asked Gabe. He's a bit of a handyman.'

'I told you he was family.'

'What do you mean?'

'Just like Cameron. He used to do things while you were out – surprise you.'

'What do you mean, *family*?'

Bubbles took out her drill, attached the plug to the socket and started to sing:

> 'I sowed the seeds of love
> And I sowed them in the spring . . .'

'Bubbles, what do you mean? Are you saying he's *related* to Cameron?'

'. . . I gather'd them up in the morning so soon
When the small birds sweetly sing . . .'

Bubbles smiled and turned on the drill, strolling around the kitchen like an assassin with a machine gun. Tina turned the power off at the socket. 'Bubbles, who is he?'

'The gardener's son was standing by
Three flowers he gave to me, me,
The pink, the blue and the violet true,
And the red, red rosy tree, tree,
And the red, red rosy tree . . .'

She seemed to have changed tunes. Tina went upstairs to the room where Gabriel had been staying. He was nowhere to be seen, but his small rucksack was packed and covered with a pullover. She opened the front pocket: a cheap wallet with a student card and two phonecards; a voucher for 10 per cent off at Pizzaland; a comb; a paperback of cartoons; a photograph of Cameron; a photograph of Tina holding a baby. She stiffened. She took the photographs – there were several – and examined them slowly. Then she heard Gabriel come in downstairs and she went to meet him. Cameron had better not have been sowing the seeds of love about.

'Sit down. Who are you?'

'I told you.'

'Who is your mother?' A note of hysteria was sounding in her voice.

'Her name's Pauline. She lives in London.'

'*Pauline? Pauline?* What sort of a name is *that*?' She could already see this woman in her head, and wanted to shake her for information.

'It's my mother's name.'

'Pauline who?'

'Canon – does it matter?'

'And she knew Cameron, didn't she?'

He looked down. 'Well, I believe so.'

'He was your father. My husband was your *father*, wasn't he?' She was pacing round the kitchen now, her nostrils wide and stiff.

'I—'

Bubbles, who was disconnecting her drill, began to sing 'The Seeds of Love' again, softly, or 'The Sprig of Thyme'.

'Your mother and Cameron had an affair, didn't they?'

'No. Absolutely not.'

'So you don't know Cameron at all?'

'No.' He looked pained. His hands were clenching the edge of the table and his knuckles were white. 'I would have liked to.'

'Why?'

'Because . . . because he sounds a nice guy, and because he was a friend of my parents way back before I was born.'

'You *knew* him?'

'No. I said no.'

'And you pretended it was just coincidence you ended up here! I think it's time you explained yourself.'

'There's nothing to say. I was going to explain and then your husband died. It didn't seem a good time to go into how we knew him.'

'How long have you been here? And how did your parents know him?'

'They were in a commune with him, back in the seventies.'

Tina calmed for a moment, and then felt more irritated than ever. 'So, do you make a habit of going through people's photographs?' She placed the photos before him on the table. He went very quiet, and seemed at a loss for an answer.

'I put them there,' said Bubbles, coming to his rescue. 'I thought he'd like a little memento.'

'You?' Tina looked at her, and so did Gabriel. She departed with her drill, muttering something about seeds and love.

Gabriel shrugged. 'Can I stay, then?'

The phone rang. It was Rhona's head teacher. Rhona had been truanting from school. Perhaps he could stay after all. She needed him in this madhouse.

The head wanted Rhona to see an educational psychologist. Did Tina realise the effect of bereavement on an eleven-year-old? Had she seen her grieve adequately yet? Could she guarantee that

Rhona would be accompanied to the school gates each morning and picked up at the end of the day?

As if on cue, Mrs Ferabee tapped on the door and strode jovially into the kitchen. With her wand in hand and her sparkling smile, she declared that *she* would see Joel and Rhona to school each day, for as long as it took Rhona to settle.

When Gabriel had taken Bubbles to the shops, Tina asked Mrs Ferabee to have a cup of tea. 'Joyce,' she said, eying her tight perm and glued-on smile and wondering if she could really have been her husband's marital confidante after a few days' acquaintance, 'do you think... do you think Cameron felt stifled?'

'*Stifled?* I'm sure he didn't. Though heaven knows, I should be the last person to know, that's for certain. He never said much more than "Hello" to me.'

'Really?' She offered her a biscuit in relief.

'You mustn't torture yourself. It was an accident. Just one of those things.'

'But he was so careful.'

'Well, he was surprised. Like I say, it was probably something to do with that person speaking to him. He got startled and—'

'What person?'

'Well, I thought he was chatting to someone—'

'What someone? You never said anything before about there being someone else there!'

'Well, there wasn't. Not for long, anyway. He ran off to phone for the ambulance – if it *was* him. It's just that I thought I heard your husband talking to someone, and he seemed surprised. It didn't last long. Didn't I mention it? It didn't seem important. Everyone was so upset and that.'

Tina looked so alert that Mrs Ferabee thought she might jump clean out of the chair and throttle her for information. 'What sort of a person?'

'I don't rightly know. A man, I suppose.'

'Young? Old?'

'Young, I reckon. I thought it was that lad of yours, Gabriel, when I met him. Obviously it can't have been, or he'd have said.'

But it was as clear as day. Gabriel had turned up earlier than he had been letting on. He had come to see Cameron: he was Cameron's love child. No wonder Cameron fell. It made her feel giddy. After Mrs Ferabee had gone she went to the front gate and waited for Gabriel to return from the Co-op with Bubbles. No wonder he'd tried to make off with the photos. He wanted a picture of his father – of course. And no wonder he felt so awkward about Rhona's crush on him. She was his sister! But he had denied it. And he didn't resemble Cameron – at least, not to look at. He did have the same way of getting things done when you weren't looking. Fixing skirting boards and transforming gardens. And he was kind to Bubbles – but then (oh lord!) she was his *grandmother*! Just then she saw him coming down the road a hundred yards off. Now she saw it clearly. Why hadn't she seen it before? The way he walked, lolloping along with uncoordinated arm and leg movements. There was absolutely no mistaking it: it was Cameron's walk.

'Tell me a little more about your parents.'

Gabriel looked awkward again. 'I told you, we don't get on much these days. I don't really want to talk about them.'

'Look, I let you into my house – a complete stranger – the least you could do is tell me who you are. Where did they meet?'

'At school, I think.'

'And they've lived in a commune with Cameron and Bubbles.'

'So I believe. I wasn't born.' Tina shot him a manic glance that said 'Aha!'

'But they weren't married then.'

'They're still not married.'

'I see. But they weren't "together" then? When they knew Cameron?'

'Oh yes. They've been together since the sixties.'

'But when you said your mother never had an affair with Cameron, that wasn't quite true, was it?'

'Yes!' Gabriel looked desperate. 'Yes! It's true!'

'But how can you *know*? You said yourself, you weren't even born!'

Gabriel was very agitated, and Tina felt sure she had hit the nail on the head.

'I *am* sure!' he wailed.

'How?'

'I just wanted to see him! I just wanted to know what he was like!'

'*How* do you know there was no affair?'

'Because my parents are two women.'

Tina stared at him.

'There you are!' he blurted. 'My parents are a couple of dykes! Happy now?'

He got up to leave the room, but Tina grabbed him by the sleeve. His pullover had a hole in it and she seemed to be unravelling him by her grasp.

'So how did they have you?' she pleaded.

'Donation sperm,' he almost whispered.

'*Cameron's?*' Her whole body seemed to shudder like a washing machine slowing down from a spin.

'He was only sixteen.'

'Your mother should've been *me*! *I* wanted Cameron's baby. I *want* his baby! *His!*' She glared at him standing limply against the sink, head down. 'Cameron's? Are you sure it was Cameron's?'

'I believe so. I'm a syringe job.' He was crying now, Tina saw. She let go of the spaghetti of navy wool in her hand and watched him make for the stairs, hiding his face.

So!

All she had ever wanted was a son by Cameron. He had left her bereft not just of a husband but of the child she would never have. He had promised her endlessly, and all the while he had given someone else a son. Some woman somewhere had borne him a son (*her* son, by rights) without ever having made love to him. Bastard.

The back door flew open and in came Rhona, ushered by Mrs Ferabee. 'All safe and well!' she sang in her high-pitched voice. 'Bye-bye, Rhona, love. See you tomorrow!'

The door closed.

'God, you know what I can't stand about that woman?' sighed Rhona. 'Why does she always have to be so bloody *happy*?'

Indeed.

Bubbles could be heard doing something with floorboards in the hallway.

'... But I refused the red rose bush
And gained the willow tree, tree,
That all the world might plainly see
How my love slighted me, me,
How my love slighted me ...'

For years she had simmered over the tables at the Happy Sausage to keep him in ringbinder files and to pay the mortgage. For years she had dropped bacon into spitting fat while he declared their home a meat-free zone. She had wiped grease off walls, coffee stains off tables and old ash out of ashtrays. She had smelt of damp rags, bleach and dripping. She had bought clothes to last. For ever. And all the while he was going to die on her.

She had put her fertility on hold, and banished her eggs into bins and sewers. She had ached inside as each possible life was frittered away, squandered by his thrift and common sense. She had answered giggly phone calls from his student friends called Zoz or Baz or Caz and wept into recycled tissues. And all the while he had a baby of his own, a baby that had been allowed to grow. A *living* boy.

At that moment she hated Cameron. She hated his death and she hated his wholegrained, multivitamined, whale-protecting life. She ran into the kitchen and flung open some cabinet doors. She pulled out a large bag of rolled oats, pierced it, and slung it on to the floor. Then she broke open a bag of mixed raisins and showered them on top. She tore out boxes of muesli, sea salt, wholegrain rice and lentils, ripping them open and flinging them on the pile. She grabbed packets of mixed pulses, alfalfa, tofu and soya protein, and tossed them into the centre of the floor. Cheeks aflame, she climbed on to the old worktop and reached for a brace of dead garlic which flaked like pot pourri in her hands. She ripped a bag of home-made cheese muslins off their hook and swept her hand along a row of bottles on a shelf. Glass phials of lavender oil, rescue remedy, olive Bach and tea-tree oil chimed to the ground. She opened a small cabinet door and wiped its shelves clean of pots and bottles filled with tablets and capsules: vitamins A, B, C, D and E, cod-liver oil, Korean ginseng, evening primrose oil, acidophyllus, synergistic selenium and cell-protective antioxidants, which bounced off the worktop and joined the growing pile on the linoleum. Next she worked her way over to another shelf, and grabbed at vegetarian cookery books called *The Gentle Lentil* and *What's Your Pulse?* and tossed them over her shoulder. She jumped down, opened another cabinet door and emptied on to the pile the contents of a bottle of extra virgin olive oil and a carton of long-life goat's milk. She marched out to the garden shed and returned with a spade, and proceeded to shovel the dripping heap into two fat binliners.

Gabriel saw her carting bags to a corner of the garden, empty them, and start a fire with paraffin. Her eyes were wild and she seemed to be moving about on springs – almost dancing.

He watched her for some time, fascinated. 'You can't start a fire there,' he told her.

She turned on him, ferocious and excited, her face, neck and cheeks bright pink. 'Why not?'

'That's my compost,' he said. The flames sprang up out of a few weak flickers, and crackled violently. She was aglow and enveloped in a wave of blurring heat. This was the woman his father had loved. He was spellbound.

Orange Blossom

The first week in June was hot. Tina took advantage of it to do some work on the roof. She stood at the top of the ladder removing broken tiles with the slater's ripper, a long flat blade with a hook at each end. She pushed the blade under the broken slates and located the hook on each nail in turn. A sharp jerk broke the nails and she could pull the slate clear. While she was up there, she bunged the top of nearby downpipes with rag to prevent debris from getting in, and began to shovel debris from the guttering. The phone ringing for the second time that morning brought her down to the kitchen.

'Now, I usually only take people from about twenty weeks,' said the woman on the phone. 'How many weeks are you?'

Tina closed her eyes and took in a deep breath: 'Nineteen.'

'Oh well, that's fine. Can you come Wednesday morning? A place has just become free.'

'Oh. Yes.'

'You know where to find me, don't you? Sarah Kelland, 18 Albach Lane.'

It was that easy. She replaced the receiver with a pulsing belly, as though this woman's belief in her pregnancy had transformed her into a real expectant mother.

On Monday she popped into Mothercare and bought a catalogue for fifty pence. She leafed through it over coffee at work, underlining the names of buggies and circling prices. When Charmain from Bathroom Fittings asked her what she was doing, she said it was for her sisters' babies. On Tuesday she visited the maternity departments and fondled the dresses. Flowered viscose, expanding trousers and floating white smocks made her choke. That evening she inspected wads of unused dress fabric in a drawer and ran up a quick pastel-flowered smock late into the night. She arrived at Sarah Kelland's the following morning looking radiant.

Sarah Kelland was a calm woman in her forties with fair-grey hair down to her waist. She sat cross-legged in grey tracksuit bottoms and a faded rust T-shirt, nodding gently as people entered her bare living room, having let themselves in through her ever-open front door.

After a while the women introduced themselves. Tina noticed how the focus of achievement differed from everyday lives. They said how many weeks they were, if it was their first baby, and talked about swollen ankles, massage potions and birthing partners. They announced their fears and expectations like children, with complete candour. There was Liz (28 weeks) who didn't show at all, and Alex (22 weeks) who looked like a boulder, Susie who was afraid of pain, and sylph-like Fiona whom Tina recognised, to her horror, as the crochet woman from outside the primary school.

'I'm Tina,' she said weakly, 'and I . . . I . . .'

'You're twenty weeks, aren't you?' helped Sarah.

'Yes.' And then to Fiona: 'Hello.'

'Do you two know each other?'

'Our children go to the same school,' said Tina.

'Oh, I don't think they do,' said Fiona, gently.

'But don't you have a child in Rhona's year?'

'Does Rhona go to Hillforth?'

Tina sagged. Hillforth was the private prep school next to the local primary. Suddenly Rhona's flopped party made sense. How many invitations had gone to complete strangers? But the class was beginning, and Sarah had them floating into their own space. There were no clocks, and time seemed endless in the pregnant capsule of her living room.

Fiona didn't go again, and Tina was to grow comfy and familiar with Liz, Susie and Alex, and with the mottled pattern on Sarah's carpet. They squatted on rubber blocks, rose wide and powerful; they rocked and swung and rolled majestically as the weeks went by, accompanied by three unknown beings who floated in the happy calm of Sarah's front room. Tina lay earthed and centred, smelling the wool of the carpet.

'Feel the baby inside you, curled up and calm. Feel yourself at one with the earth. Touch your baby. Stroke it . . . feel how it must feel . . . warm and dark . . . hearing your breath and your voice . . . floating inside you . . .'

Tina paid a visit to a department store on the way home and bought a fleece sleepsuit in pastel green.

On the weekend Andy took them both for a walk in the hills with his dog, Roger. Tina was relieved to have the extra company, as Rhona kept up a babble of conversation with Andy, and Roger was amenable to having sticks thrown for him, acting as an excellent focus for her own attention. She threw Roger a forked twig and he scampered over to a beautiful quarry that shone golden in the early evening sun. Set in the green hillside, it looked as if someone had taken a bite out of a giant apple. Tina ran after him to admire the yellow stone and escape her suitor. When she re-joined the path she saw that Rhona had cajoled Andy into clambering up to a sheer drop to see a local landmark: a tall formation of stone that teetered on the hillside overlooking Moorhampton and the Severn Valley. Their voices had become distant and tinny, and she could no longer hear their conversation.

'I don't suppose you're too happy about Tina going out with men,' he said, taking in the view.

Rhona looked across at the sky, fading mauve and pale over the Black Mountains which rose like dark clouds where the land met the sky. 'Oh, I am. Provided you're good at DIY.'

'So that's important to you, is it?' he smiled. 'Why's that?'

'You haven't seen our house! At least, not properly. It's a shell. Dad bought it to do it up. Are you any good at that sort of thing?'

'Hey, hang on! I don't get the impression she's that struck on me. I have the feeling—'

'But *that's* the way to her heart!' She looked over her shoulder to check that Tina was out of sight. 'Come round some time when she's at work. All the floorboards need replacing and the place needs rewiring. We can't afford it, and I just *know* she's going to try it herself and we'll all be blown up. You're an electrician, aren't you?'

'A *technician.*'

'Same difference, isn't it? You must know a bit about it.

They stood and watched as the sun sank over Gloucester, and bled into the horizon, somewhere in Wales. Andy looked thoughtful, and watched his dog padding after Tina beneath them on the path.

When Tina came home from work on Monday she was tugged by the sleeve into the living room. Rhona made a mock bugle call and turned a smart golden knob on the wall. The light came on slowly, and grew brighter as Rhona turned. And it wasn't from the centre of the ceiling either, but from pairs of bulbs on the walls with frosted glass shades. Tina stared as she was pulled into the hall and up the stairs for the same experience.

'How did you . . .? Who . . .?'

'Andy! Isn't it great?'

Tina's nostrils began to move. They widened and hardened, and she breathed as if she were trying to blow out a candle with her nose.

'Aren't you pleased?'

'Pleased? How *dare* he! Who does he think he is?'

Rhona sighed, 'Oh, well!' and went off to the fridge for a yoghurt. She wasn't a bit bothered by Tina's reaction. If she played her cards right, the next man might do the flooring.

But David, the next date, was a computer software manager whose only experience of carpentry was a rocking chair made of pegs when he was nine. He was very perplexed at the prospect of re-flooring, and opted for painting the windows instead. Rhona let him off, but Tina was furious. 'What's *wrong* with these men? Why do they have to *interfere*?'

'I don't know,' said Rhona. 'I *told* him you wouldn't like it,' and she slunk off to play with Joel.

Gareth was a different kettle of fish. Tina quite liked him, and Rhona wasn't sure if she should intervene. But she gave them a week, and at the first sign of dissatisfaction from Tina she gave him the flooring. Coming home from work early one day, Tina was met by the sight of Gareth sweating and sawing at a trestle with sticking plasters all over his hands, and Rhona sitting cross-legged in a pile of sawdust reading instructions to him from a DIY manual. He had used the tongued-and-grooved boards that Cameron had already bought, but he hadn't shaved off the tongues of the edging boards and there were gaps around the floor which were made worse by his having sawn off the lengths jaggedly. To top it all, he hadn't fixed the boards to the joists underneath, but had tapped nails in haphazardly across the floor in some sort of diagonal pattern which he clearly found pleasing, with no regard for water pipes or wiring underneath. Most of the nails stood proud of the boards, and it looked like some kind of primitive torture room.

By the time she dated Arwell, a heating engineer ('Ideal!' thought Rhona), Tina was demanding reassurances beforehand that he would not, in any circumstances, touch the house. Utterly bewildered, Arwell gave up after a week, more attracted by another video at the agency of a bosomy Piscean called Cressida who liked curries. It was then that Rhona pounced. He couldn't possibly leave them in this mess: they were both so cut up, the very least he could do was fit a new boiler for the central heating.

When Paul came along, Tina refused to introduce Rhona. Paul was a little man with a big car. He had an Audi A6 Quattro with a 2.8 litre 172BHP V6 SOHC engine with twin airbags, ABS, cruise control and air conditioning, and capable of 0–60 miles per hour in 8.1 seconds. Before that he had owned a Mazda MX6 with 2.5 litre V6 engine, and next he was going to buy a BMW M5 with 3.8 litre V6 engine, anti-lock brakes, side impact bars, air conditioning and traction control, which would go from 0–60 in 5.6 seconds. Not that he only had one car, mind. He had two others: one was an MGB GT and he bet she couldn't guess what the other one was.

Nope.

But she was getting the hang of this dating lark now, and knew that a meeting followed by a date was the least you could get away with politely. She agreed to a meal out, and when he asked her about Rhona, she thought it might not be such a bad idea, after all, to take her along.

Keith Pooley was stocktaking and thinking about life. There was nothing like the different colours of emulsion paint to set him day-dreaming, and at Dream Peach he gazed towards the day-light in the foyer and thought he saw Tina Morrison. When he first saw her, Keith had been quite attracted to her. But then he had been struck by her hardness. There seemed to him a greyness surrounding her sometimes, a lack of colour. She had just lost a husband, but she never showed any signs of emotion. And the way she wanted to do everything herself, without even the most well-intentioned help. He wished he could draw her out a bit, but he never knew what to say to people in grief. He had once told Linda 'It could have been worse' when she lost her father, but that hadn't seemed to make things better. He was pretty certain it wouldn't help Tina. If he had just once caught her crying, or even shouting, he might have been able to warm to her more. But she seemed further away from him than Linda, who was on the other side of the Atlantic.

Something had happened, though, to set him thinking about her again. The way that lad had looked at him . . . He knew there was something odd going on, and he didn't want Tina getting hurt. No way.

He had always wished he could be more adventurous, less fearful of travel and leaving things. Sometimes he re-invented himself as an adventuring hero like Harrison Ford or Clint Eastwood. He would find himself in different locations on the globe and feel quite at home amidst palm trees or swamps or tundra. He would be immune to mosquitoes or frostbite or whatever, and eat chicken heads or raw fish with the natives without so much as an indigestion tablet. He had imaginary interviews with TV presenters and answered questions with a fluency he only possessed in his head. No, of course he hadn't been frightened hanging off that horse in the stampede scene; it was no big deal – any man could have done it if he didn't mind a bit of bruising. What? No, he hadn't used a stunt man for the burning motorbike chase: that had been him in flames – there was nothing to it if you kept your head. Yeah, it was a bit hairy the helicopter incident. He *had* said his prayers hanging on to the undercarriage when it swooped so close to the rock face, but it was all in a day's work. He imagined women of every nationality trying to be close to him. He would kneel on the floor with an almond-eyed girl in Japan, surrounded by paper walls, or save a beautiful Creole girl from certain death, or lie in a wigwam with a squaw who smelt of suede. But in the end they all transformed themselves into Linda; Linda in a different costume with different hair and eyes. But always it was her somehow.

And he knew that he never *could* go to any of these places, unless he was completely anaesthetised first. He had only been on two plane journeys in his life, and each one had been a disaster. Even as he reached Heathrow he began to feel homesick for all he had left behind; on the first trip with Linda it was just his house, his relatives and his allotment. That had been the honeymoon. On the second trip, many years later, they left their little daughter Carol with her grandparents and went away for a week. As the plane circled London and then rose steeply on that cloudless summer day he felt nauseous. Life as he knew it grew smaller and smaller and he felt it tugging at his stomach like an enormous magnet. By the time he saw white cliffs and sea from the window he felt he might suddenly be propelled back to earth like something stretched very long and tight on an elastic band. But it didn't happen, and he was choked and powerless as he thought of the small girl he had been separated from by thousands of miles of air and ocean. What if she were crying right then? What if something awful happened to her and he couldn't get back in time to save her? When Linda ordered them a bucks fizz he felt as though he had been turned to clay. He could hardly hold the plastic beaker and the bubbles jabbed at his throat like needles. Linda seemed all bubble, and that only accentuated the leaden feeling he would have for days.

Was that Rhona in the foyer? Perhaps not; she was gone now, anyway. He watched the children in the foyer round the rocking aeroplane and the wooden horse. Small children itched and squabbled to get astride the horse, and once there they just sat, bewildered by the lack of action, surveying the world from a new status. Keith marvelled at their willingness to assume adult roles. They wanted to be grown-ups, to ride aeroplanes and animals and tackle the world. It happened so slowly, the loss of enthusiasm for such toys. One day you saw wooden donkeys and trains with flashing lights and you realised you felt no excitement. You didn't have to pretend any more, you didn't have to practise at being a grown-up. And yet the sad thing was, Keith Pooley never had needed to know how to pilot a plane and he never did ride bareback into a small town in the Wild West. All that practice for nothing. He wanted to go over and tell the children in the foyer they were wasting their time, but he knew it was kinder to let them be duped.

Strawberry Fool

Keith Pooley was in a dither. He had received a letter from Linda after nearly eleven years of silence, saying that she was coming to England in two weeks' time and would like to see him. Would she bring his daughter? Would he see Carol as a thirteen-year-old? What would she look like now? What would she think of him? How was he going to impress them? He couldn't think straight for questions. He had just sixteen days to prepare for the most momentous occasion of his life so far and he felt inadequate. He asked Tina Morrison which would be the most impressive restaurant to take them to.

'The Yew Tree, if you want to spend a fortune.'

'I do.'

'But if you ask me, a thirteen-year-old would prefer a burger bar.'

'Oh, do you reckon?'

'Now, Parkers' Brasserie is good. You can get posh stuff, but chips as well if you want.'

'Is it, you know . . . romantic?'

'Oh yes. Candles and that.'

'Hmmm.' He stroked his chin and went to ask Stephanie on Customer Services.

He was supposed to be putting in some orders for paints, but he couldn't keep his mind on anything. He kept going back to the letter, and in particular to those two sentences. He took it out of his pocket, the limp airmail paper corrugated with heavy biro: 'We plan to come over on the 20ith (thats July), and I would like to see you again for a chat, specially about you're daughter. Their have been some big changes in are lives.' He folded it up and slipped it into his blue overall.

He had six hundred pounds saved up towards an extension on the house. He would do it himself, of course, but the money would barely cover materials. And there was that activity holiday he was planning next Easter: climbing in Wales for singles. Well, all that would have to go on hold. It sounded as though she had split up with this Steve bloke and was seeking some sort of stable future for their daughter. Everything depended on impressing her, and he would have to think carefully how this money would be best spent. He would just have time to repaint the rendering on the front of the house and maybe to fit the new bathroom earlier than planned. He would have to keep her away from the house as much as possible (it being the one she walked out of for its cheapness so many years ago), but still, if she *had* to see it, he felt sure she would be impressed by the changes in *his* life too: for example, the 80 per cent wool carpet in the living room, the built-in television and stereo system and the fitted kitchen with mixer tap and double drainer.

He was doing some calculations in his head when he thought he saw Rhona again through the glass in the foyer. He stood up and squinted in the direction of the doors. There was no mistaking Rhona with her thick spectacles and flossy hair, peering in from behind the children's rocker jets.

He felt certain that if he approached her she would disappear again, so he decided to take an alternative route to the foyer and enter it by a side door. He came up beside her and stood perfectly still as he watched her pressed up against the glass.

'Hello, Rhona.'

Rhona turned, startled. She eyed the automatic exit door furtively.

'I thought it was you,' he said softly. 'And I'm glad you're here because I want to ask you some advice.'

'Fire away,' she said, looking relieved.

He sat down on a yellow slatted bench and patted the space next to him for her to join him. 'Well, now. Point is, I want to impress someone very much, and I don't know where to start.'

Rhona skewed her mouth to one side and looked pensive. 'Depends who it is, really.'

'Well, truth is, my wife upped and left me eleven year ago and she took my little girl with her. Now, she's coming to see me soon and . . . well, you never know, she might bring our Carol back to me.'

'Eleven years?' Rhona's eyes grew wide and her heavy spectacles slipped a little. 'You mean you haven't seen her since I was *born*?'

'That's about it. Yes. There 'tiz.'

'So, you want to impress your daughter so she'll want to come and live with you?'

'Well . . . now there's a thing.' He looked off into the middle distance. 'Now there's a thing.'

'Or do you want to impress your wife so she'll marry you again?'

Keith hadn't expected such a blunt summing up of his thought processes, but it was pretty much correct. 'I was thinking of dining out, maybe.'

Rhona scratched her neck. 'How long are they coming for?'

'Here? Just a day or two – and it may just be Linda, my ex-wife.'

'Hmmm. Well, take your wife somewhere adulty. You know – nightclub or some such, and candlelit dinner. And take your daughter to Pizzaland.'

'Pizzaland?'

'Yes, definitely.' She looked quite satisfied with her summary. 'Or anywhere with strawberry milkshakes and chips.'

Keith Pooley thanked her for her help and asked her if she shouldn't perhaps be in school. The question seemed to transform her. A small furrow appeared above her glasses and she looked away from him. He knew suddenly that it was Rhona he had seen some days ago, and that she had been there every day, lurking, just looking in. He felt a sudden pang of sadness for her, and was irritated by his utter inability to help her.

'I get very lonely sometimes,' he said. She said nothing and examined her battered nails. 'I expect you get lonely too.'

She looked at him unexpectedly, seeming to plead for something. 'Do you sometimes just want to check if your daughter's safe?'

He looked back at the clear eyes and tried to measure his words. 'I do. I'd have given anything to hear news about her over these years – or better still, see her – even just from afar, just so's I'd know, like.'

'But I *can*.'

'How's that, then?'

'I *can* check on Mum. I just need to come here every day and see she's safe. I know it sounds silly, but I need to know that she's alive. She's all I've got now. I lost my real mum, and now my dad, and—' Her eyes began to fill with tears. 'She mustn't die – I've got to make sure she isn't dying!'

Keith Pooley pulled a Kleenex from his pocket and offered it to her as though she might fall apart if he touched her. She took it, buried her head in his shoulder and started to shake. He tentatively put an arm around her and said he understood. And the thing was, he did.

He was filled with tenderness for the little girl in the foyer and wanted to do something more for her than offer her a shoulder. With nothing else to hand he gave her a Did-It-Myself biro and a dog-eared but unused headed notepad from his pocket. He promised to keep an eye on Tina for her and was about to phone for a taxi to take her back to school when something stopped him dead in his tracks.

A woman in a long cream dress with swathes of silk chiffon minced in through the automatic doors on very high-heeled gold sandals. She was teetering across the foyer to the main entrance when she spotted Keith Pooley to her right, standing by a payphone.

'Keith?'

There was an odd silence. They both looked each other up and down quickly.

'Wow!' said the woman, breaking into a heavily made-up smile of rose-hip red. 'I can't believe it! You look *just* the same!'

She had a curious west country accent tinged with American, and now that he'd had time to take her in, Keith Pooley knew she was his ex-wife, Linda.

'Linda! I wasn't expecting you for another fortnight,' he said. He was breathing heavily and the back of his neck turned a deep pink. All of a sudden he was aware of his hands. He didn't know where to put them. They kept bouncing out of his pockets, skidding off his chin or his hair, and seemed to have expanded in size to take up the entire foyer with their clumsiness. But just as the long fingers had pretty much settled into a ring-fumbling knot, he was almost thrown backwards by the appearance of a second person.

'Hi,' said an American girl with long limbs and a deep tan. 'Long time no see.'

She had a long blonde bob and held out a hand barbed with frosted nails. He clasped it, cool and smooth in his own bunch of jittery, damp fingers. Could this really be – just an arm's length away – his own little daughter?

'Carol?'

'Carol?'

'She's called Michelle now,' interjected the cream woman.

'Michelle?' He swallowed. 'Well!' He swallowed again, his eyebrows raised right up into his hair. 'Well!'

Michelle withdrew her hand politely, rubbed it briefly on her jeans, and looked at the tall man with jug-handled ears who stood before her like a grovelling fan. 'I guess I've changed,' she said.

'Yes. Yes, but you've turned out real pretty. Well I never!'

'Michelle and I are just in this part of the world for a couple of days – I'm seeing my mother.' (Her mother was Mrs Tilley! This woman was related to Mrs Tilley who had worked at the Co-op for twenty years and who still lived down Vivian Way on the council estate near the 'Danger: Electricity' pylon.)

'So you'll not be staying?'

'Only two nights. We had to catch an earlier flight.'

Keith did not know which of them to look at. He needed to study them both a great deal. There was a waft of perfume in the air from one of them, or maybe a mixture from both of them. At any rate, he felt dizzy from its smell and seemed to reel about on the spot, eyes wide open, mouth ajar, panting like a dog about to go for a walk.

'So when shall we go for our meal? I mean, you would like a meal, I suppose?'

'That's what I called to see you about,' said Linda. 'It'll have to be tomorrow night, if that's OK.'

'Fine!' he said, too hastily by half. 'Fine – I expect. I'll have to consult my diary.' He made to pull something out of his pocket, and realised he had only his wallet and an order book full of carbon paper. He hastily patted an empty pocket and chuckled nervously. 'No – I'm sure tomorrow night will be fine. Now, where would you like to go?' He looked at the girl and said, 'No expense spared, mind. Anywhere you like! Though I expect you'd maybe like somewhere with strawberry milkshakes and chips!'

'Strawberry milkshake? Yuk!' said Michelle. 'And *chips*?'

'French fries,' said her mother, smiling benevolently. 'No, Michelle won't be coming.'

'Oh. But shan't I see you?' He looked at Michelle in panic.

'I'm going to Oxford to see some friends.'

'Oxford? On your own? Is that a good idea?'

'Dad's driving me over. He knows some folks who live there.'

Dad? Her *dad*? Keith began to panic. She didn't want his strawberry milkshake and she didn't want him.

'But don't you know who I am?'

'Oh, sure. But I was too young to remember you.'

'Am I . . . what you expected?'

'Sure. You're exactly how Mom's always described you. I didn't believe her, but you're even more like she said than I expected.' The girl was smiling benignly. Keith did not want to be described by his ex-wife. It was like having your arch-enemy write your CV. He didn't want to be consigned to history under some grotesque character reference she had sketched of him. But Linda was giving him her phone number at a hotel and they were turning to go. His daughter was turning away from him after eleven years. Not being *taken* away this time. *Turning away*.

'Look – don't go! Won't you let me show you round? See where I work?'

He waved a hand at the store behind him, and Michelle glanced at the rows of paints, screws, locks and wood finishes without emotion.

'I think I'll take a rain check on that one,' she said.

Keith had no idea what a rain check was, but he felt she was rejecting him. He was about to reach out to her, pull her towards him, rock her to and fro as he had when she had last been in his arms, all wide-eyed and adoring, when something happened.

All of a sudden Rhona darted at him from the yellow bench and thrust her Did-It-Myself pen and notepad under his nose.

'You're Keith Pooley, aren't you? I *thought* it was you. Oh, please, *please* can I have your autograph?'

He froze in shock, aware only that the incident had made the two women turn back to look.

'I—'

'Are you *famous*?' asked Michelle.

'I—'

'Of *course* he is,' said Rhona, pityingly. 'Where have you *been*? Haven't you heard of Keith Pooley? The famous singer and songwriter?'

Keith licked his lips nervously.

'Oh, he's into everything,' said Rhona. 'Rock, heavy metal, jazz. You name it. He's even written songs for When. Haven't you heard of them in the States?'

'Well, yes I have,' said Michelle, smiling in surprised recognition.

'Michelle wants to be a singer,' said Linda, uncertain whether or not to be impressed. 'Perhaps you could pull a few strings?'

'A few strings?' yelped Rhona. 'He could get you a record contract, I should think, with *his* connections.' Then she turned to Keith again. '*Please* give me your autograph – just write "To Rhona".'

Keith was way out of his depth now, and took the pen in fingers which seemed to have turned into bananas. Michelle was interested, but Linda was steering her away. 'We must go. We have to visit the shops and the taxi's waiting in the car park.'

Keith reached into his wallet and produced all that he had: two ten pound notes. He presented them to Michelle. 'Here, buy yourself a little something on me.' She took them and said 'Thanks', looking at them as though trying to work out the exchange rate for dollars. He hated himself for those two ragged notes. If only he had known they were coming today he could have produced a crisp fifty pound note or even two or – hell – a dozen. Why not? She was worth everything he had.

'Can't I see you before you go?' he asked, looking at Michelle. 'The Yew Tree, tomorrow night?'

'I'll be there,' said Linda, answering for her. 'Maybe Michelle can call in for an *hors d'oeuvre.*' (She pronounced it 'orduvruh' with her strange hybrid accent.) And they whisked themselves away through the automatic doors, leaving a thin scent of vanilla.

Lemon Sorbet

'Can you come round and play after tea?' Joel stood with his toes on the edge of the kitchen doorstep, his heels rocking precariously in empty space.

'Sorry, I can't. Got to go out with Mum and a man who talks about cars.'

'Oh, well.'

'Hey, I found out some more about Wig. You'll never guess! But you mustn't tell anyone. Promise?'

'I promise.'

'Seems his parents are a couple of lesbians! Bubbles told me, and then Mum said it was true.'

'Oh.'

'You don't know what a lesbian is, do you?'

'I do!'

Rhona looked at Joel who was kicking the step and scuffing his shoes. 'Are you a lesbian, then?' she asked.

'I'm not saying.'

'Are you or aren't you?'

He felt cornered. 'I may be. Who wants to know?'

Rhona looked mischievous. 'You've got to say either yes or no.'

He looked at her large clear blue eyes and her thin face. It was clearly important to her; he couldn't sit on the fence on this one. He was desperate.

'Yes, then. Yes I am, actually.'

A smile spread over her face. Then she threw her arms around him and gave him a resounding kiss.

* * *

The restaurant was quiet when Paul, Tina and Rhona arrived, and a boy with a dinner jacket and a lovebite showed them to some pink velvet sofas next to the bar. Rhona looked intrigued and wondered where the tables were, but Paul seemed quite at home, ordering drinks for everyone and asking about today's specials.

'And is the salmon Scottish?' he asked.

'Um . . . I'll just go and ask.'

The boy came back, smiling. 'It is, sir.'

'And is there a choice of mushrooms?'

'There is, sir.' He listed a selection of fungi that sounded like racehorses, while Tina looked on in awe.

They studied the menus.

The waiter took Rhona's order first, but she was quite unable to decipher anything edible, and didn't want to be told what to have. She gave the waiter an informed look and asked, 'Are the vegetables organically grown?'

'Uh . . . I can find out,' said the waiter. Tina glared at her, decided to have whatever Paul had, and wondered if she had lipstick on her teeth. Rhona ordered snails, just for a laugh.

After ten minutes they were ushered into a low-lit room with square tables, each with two starched tablecloths and heavy silver cutlery. Tina and Rhona gawped as the waiter poured a thimbleful of wine into a tall glass for Paul, and he tasted it. He looked as though he were trying to suck out some food that had got stuck between his teeth, and while he was deliberating on his response three people were ushered to the table next to theirs: a slim girl in faded denim jeans who moved like a model, a glamorous woman in her mid-thirties and a tall, dark, quite attractive man.

'Keith!' said Tina before she could stop herself. He was clearly with his ex-wife and daughter, and she was afraid their closeness might be uncomfortable for him.

'Tina?' said Keith, seeming to need a second look. 'Hi! . . . This is Linda and . . . er . . . Michelle.' He gestured to them proudly, and Tina stood up to shake hands. Linda and Michelle remained seated, examining her, and Tina felt foolish and clumsy. Linda was looking at her evening dress as though she could see it was from the Age Concern nearly new shop four Christmases ago.

Linda's hand was cold with rings when she shook it, and her daughter's was cool and skeletal with painted nails, each a perfect oval. Linda's face was wide, radiant and framed with orange-gold hair that did what she wanted it to. A few faint freckles showed through her tan, and her reckless red lipstick bled slightly into the tiniest of lines around her mouth. The whites of her eyes were almost blue, and set off a pair of dazzling pale green irises which darted about and fixed now on Tina like spotlights. The daughter seemed mellow in comparison, or perhaps she was just bored. Grey-eyed and velvet-skinned, she arranged her limbs on the table like ornaments, entwining her tan willowy arms with her hands pointing to the ceiling, displaying an array of bracelets and charms. Tina wanted to go and sit somewhere else, but knew that would seem rude. She returned to her table, barely a yard away, where Paul had just agreed to the wine being poured and Rhona had ducked behind a wine list.

'Rhona, sit up straight and behave.' But Rhona had no intention of letting Linda and Michelle see that Keith's greatest fan was already known to him.

Keith had not expected to meet anyone he knew at the Yew Tree, but least of all Tina. Had she known he would be there? Had Rhona told her it was tonight? It was unlikely that Rhona would have mentioned their meeting earlier in the foyer as she should have been in school. But what shocked him most of all was Tina's appearance. When she had said 'Keith!' he had turned to see a woman clad in deep burgundy with shapely bare shoulders. As she bent over to shake hands with his family, he noticed the softest mousse of hair at the nape of her neck under her carefully pleated and pinned up soft curls. He had never seen her out of overalls or uniform, always a vague, formless figure in blue. Now she seemed transformed. His excitement at being with Linda and Michelle gave the evening a heightened, surreal air, and he could feel his body literally swell with pride as he introduced them. 'And this is Tina – a very good friend.' His ribcage seemed to expand as if a giant fluttering bird were pressing it out from the inside. He hadn't banked on the look of curiosity – or even jealousy – on Linda's face as Tina smiled. He hadn't banked on Tina's shoulder and the fabric of her dress brushing his ear as she stood up straight and returned to her chair. He wondered if the thrill from that inch of velvet and skin were simply part of the magic of this evening. But after it, he breathed deeply into his chest and felt like Clint Eastwood.

He had insisted on their first course being prompt to allow Michelle to leave for Oxford at a quarter to nine. The *hors d'oeuvre* arrived: two square inches of something-or-other on a leaf. Keith looked at it. He hovered with his fork, waiting for Linda to start, wondering if this was enough to keep Michelle here until eight forty-five. But Michelle asked about his connections, and seemed happy to bombard him with questions about who he knew. He was conscious that Tina could hear easily from the next table, and felt in a quandary: he was unable to lie and unable to tell the truth. He knew he held Michelle on the finest of threads; one disillusionment and she would be lost for ever. He picked up the decorated whatnot with his fork and swallowed it whole.

'Well now,' he replied, when he had finished chewing, and 'Let's see—' and he was relieved when the waiter removed his plate and plonked a sorbet in front of him. He picked up a spoon and watched as the others started to eat. He held his hand up to his wife. 'Stop!' he said loudly.

The waiter came over and said, 'Is everything all right, sir?'

'We haven't had our main course, yet,' he said. 'And I don't think I ordered an ice cream.'

He looked over to Linda – 'Did *you*?' – but Linda was smiling, and Michelle giggled, 'You're a gas!'

'This is just a sorbet, sir, to clean your palate between courses.'

'Oh,' said Keith, feeling himself redden. 'So it's free, like?'

'Certainly, sir.'

He could feel Linda's sympathy oozing over the table towards him. Poor, small town Keith. He could sense Michelle realised he hadn't been joking, and saw from the corner of his eye that both Tina and her very smart date had heard it all. He couldn't see Tina's face as she was facing the same way as him, but he could see the man opposite her smirking. They were sipping wine and hadn't been brought their first course. Their waiter had disappeared into the kitchen, and only a skinny waitress leant over a distant table collecting plates. Her uniform was made for someone altogether larger, and her dark stockinged legs seemed to have no calves. Tina's date put down his wineglass, raised an arm imperiously and snapped his fingers. 'Service! Service!'

The waitress continued balancing plates on her arm. The smart man clicked his fingers again and she turned and called over to him, 'It takes more than two fingers to make me come, mate!'

'Dawn!' cried Tina in delight.

'Tina!' yelled Dawn, bounding over with plates teetering on her arm.

Keith cleared his throat. Linda and Michelle were looking at Tina, and clearly associating her with trash after all.

'And look at *you* all growed up, little madam,' said Dawn, pulling the wine list from Rhona's face and exposing an apologetic, frozen smile.

'Well, say something, Rhona!' said Tina. 'Has the cat got your tongue?'

Michelle chuckled. 'Well look at that! It's your greatest fan, Keith, sitting right next to your dear friend. Ain't that just a coincidence?' She looked at him, and he was charred. He could feel Clint Eastwood slinking off.

'Well! Keith Pooley, you just never change!' sighed Linda, clearly remembering the fact that he never did introduce her to George Best (even though he'd never promised). Her eyes suddenly lit up as a waiter ushered in a blond-haired man in a long, cashmere jacket.

'Dad!' said Michelle. 'I'm all ready. Shall we go?' and she gathered up a tan leather bag and ran her hand through her pale hair. Keith, hungry for a few more moments, tried to drink in everything about her. He noticed the blonde down at her hairline before the hair flopped slowly back into place, and some faint freckles beneath the tan on her nose. He saw the crystal blue eyes smiling out at another man – a pretender – and cheeks so young and soft they had barely changed since he used to wipe fruit purée off them. He stood up suddenly. 'Don't go!'

The waiter had already brought Michelle her jacket, and feigned a polite deafness. Michelle turned back to the table. 'I'll see you tomorrow, then, Mom. Keith – nice to meet you. I'm sure we'll run into each other again some time.'

Keith stood immobile as Michelle was escorted to the door at the end of the dark room. She seemed to disappear into the shadows and he had no way of reaching her.

'*Please!*' he called after her, but she was gone.

'Oh, sit down!' said Linda. 'And let's get on with the meal. I've got things to discuss.'

To his left the waitress had disappeared and Tina's table seemed to have reassembled itself. Tina herself was very quiet, and he could hear the smart man talking about side impact protection.

Tangerine Dream

Rhona appeared in the foyer again the following day, and Keith spotted her just as she was turning away towards the car park. 'Rhona? That you?'

She seemed relieved to see him. She wanted to apologise, but didn't know how. She had wondered all night how he would appear. Or perhaps he would have taken an overdose and no one would wonder where he was for days. Then she would go to his house and find him lying on the floor with the curtains closed, clutching at Linda's letter or photographs of Michelle as a baby. Or the cause of death might be a broken heart: she had heard of people dying of broken hearts, and had almost witnessed it last night in the restaurant. Keith had seemed to crumble on the spot and said very little for the rest of the evening. When they had left there was no light in his eyes when he smiled goodbye. He had died inside if not in real life and it was all her fault. She had let him down at the most important moment of his life and he would never forgive her. She couldn't measure the tone of his voice, and almost wished he would shout at her.

'Rhona? You all right?'

She looked at his anxious face and her eyes filled with tears. 'Oh, Mr Pooley!' She ran over to him and clutched at the tall blue overall.

'Now just you tell me all about it,' he said, and to his dismay she cried even more loudly.

'It's *you* I'm worried about,' she sniffled at last. 'I broke your heart.'

He stroked her head and felt a rope bridge had been thrown out to him from an opposite precipice. He stood and smiled for a very long time. People passing through the foyer thought he was selling double glazing. Then he said, 'Come on, I'll walk you back to school.'

They walked across the car park and talked for twenty minutes about people they missed. As they rounded the corner to the main road, Rhona reached up and took his hand. He took it, dizzy with surprise and joy. He felt someone had thrown him a life jacket.

If Tina had not emptied her handbag on to the kitchen table to throw out all the address cards, she might never have met him. Leafing through them over the rubbish bin, dropping them one by one, she came across *Carl Salter: Therapist* in Arwell's broken handwriting. She frowned; which one was he? Then she remembered Arwell's recommendation for bereavement counselling. She looked at the phone, afraid of having to talk in a group with people who knew how to talk, afraid of discovering she was doing everything wrong with Rhona. But visions of Moorhampton primary school pavement crashed in on her thoughts. Those mothers with their fresh lime juice recipes and swivel wheel integral basket pushchairs, looking askance at the woman who hadn't dealt with it properly, whose daughter needed some sort of behavioural therapy because she hadn't agreed to counselling.

Carl Salter popped round for a chat on his way to somewhere, and reassured her on every count. The heavy black lashes rocked up and down over the deep blue eyes like dolls' lids. She was hooked.

'Good health care is a *sine qua non* where bereavement is concerned.'

'Is it?'

'Yeah. You can't carry your child's grief for her, you know; you can only help her to express it. And a good network of support for *you* is essential too.'

'Oh well, then.'

The first group meeting on Thursday was frightening. Complete strangers talked fluently about their feelings, and some cried openly. Tina wanted to know how to get to sleep at night, not why Rupert was subconsciously angry with his dead wife for not finishing his pullover. But 'sleep' was in two weeks' time, and she supposed it was worth waiting for, so long as no one made her talk about Cameron in the meantime. By the end of the evening she felt that some compulsive talkers had resolved their own grief by exporting it to her, and she secretly vowed not to go again.

Until the phone rang, and Carl invited her out for a drink that same evening.

He took her to a brasserie she had never heard of with red velveteen tablecloths and live music. A short man in a T-shirt was playing a saxophone, and a long-haired man stood in his own spotlight shaking maracas from time to time.

Tina liked Carl. He had a psychology degree, a qualification in homoeopathy, and had trained in T'ai Chi, Past Life Healing and aromatherapy. He cooked for himself and mended his own clothes and could say foreign things like *déjà vu*. His eyebrows ran in two straight dark lines across his brow, which was hooded and angular like the raincover of a pram. His hair – thick and dark – was not unlike Cameron's, and the way he ran his hand through it from time to time reminded her of Cameron preening when he wanted to look his best. His nose was as straight as a statue's, and his teeth sat well in his mouth like a row of piano keys. Everything about him seemed capable, from the way he smiled to the way he ordered the drinks.

She wasn't going to get all excited, though. *Ho* no. She was not in the mood for romance. She was still jittery about all the unmatching pieces of her life, conscious of something still jarring on the nerves, a sense of disorder. But Carl asked her so many questions that she began to unwind. What did she like most about her life at present? What did she like least? What made her happy? She thought of writing them down for Julia and Gerald at the agency. The saxophone was deep and throaty in the background. It was impossible not to melt a little.

'Doing up a house? Now *that's* an interesting hobby. Of course, you realise the house represents oneself. You know – basement equals the unconscious and where we keep memories of traumatic events in our lives; the attic is the intellect; chimney the birth canal – or is that the hallway? Anyhow, you know the kind of thing: front door, public persona; opening windows, letting people see your feelings. Where do you spend most of your time, I wonder?'

'Oh, well. The kitchen, I suppose. It's the only room that's livable in.'

'Excellent! Creativity. Mother role. Nurturing.'

'Oh.'

The music was loud enough to replace a longer response.

'What do *you* do?' she asked at last. 'I mean, what do you actually *do*?'

'Well, I'm a counsellor mostly.'

Ah! She wasn't going to look stupid this time. 'Which party?'

He laughed and said, 'Very good!' She chuckled nervously, but her face was still a question mark.

'I'm not political,' he smiled. 'I do therapy sessions almost full-time: broken relationships, bereavement, dream therapy, self-awareness.'

'Oh. Of course.'

The long-haired man shook his maracas once and hid behind a curtain of hair to wait for the next momentous occasion.

At ten past one the next day the head rang from Rhona's school and told Tina to come and fetch her straight away. She had been found in possession of cannabis and was 'drug-pushing' in the playground.

Tina had just started her lunch-hour decorating. She plonked her paintbrush in some Polyclens and ran to school. She was directed to a newly carpeted room smelling of rubber underlay, and she stood in the doorway in her paint-spattered overalls. Rhona was staring at the ground and sucking her top lip. The head, a young ginger-haired woman with no neck, remained seated as she entered.

'Wrong door!' she said. Tina hovered, and opened her mouth to speak, but the woman sighed heavily. 'Down the corridor, second on the left.'

'Oh.'

'They were delivered over an hour ago.'

'What were?'

'The breeze blocks and cement bags.'

'Oh.' Tina stood still, confused. 'That's nice, then.'
'Well, go *on*! Second on the left and jump to it!'
Tina made to go, and then turned back hesitantly. 'I'll just—'
'Mrs Stacey,' said Rhona soberly. 'This is my mother.'

Rhona was still looking at the same piece of carpet half an hour later.

'I think you should know,' Mrs Stacey was saying, 'that we are very sympathetic to your circumstances, and clearly we don't want to expel Rhona – given that her . . . given what she's been through – but we cannot allow this sort of thing. She's already involved Joel Ferabee and he's a *sweet* little boy. I'd like you to let her see our educational psychologist' – she turned to Rhona – 'just for a chat,' and then back to Tina: 'These things need to be talked through. Has she had anyone to talk it all over with?'

'Well, I think . . . I've been at work . . .'

'Sometimes it helps to have a bit of professional support to go through the traumatic aspects of bereavement. It's still very early days, and we've noticed her grief has not been worked out.'

'Oh.'

'And this difficult behaviour has been getting worse, hasn't it, Rhona?'

Rhona smiled with one half of her face, but her eyes were red and glazed. She nodded, and seemed unable to stop.

'I'd like you to go home with your mother, Rhona, and tell her what you haven't been able to tell me.' She indicated some roll-ups on her desk and turned back to Tina. 'We were about to call a doctor. Could you do that when you get home? Have her checked over? I don't know how much of this stuff she's had.'

On her way home, Rhona couldn't feel her legs, so Tina drove her straight to casualty. The doctor wanted to keep her in overnight until they could find out exactly what she'd taken. Tina was panic-stricken. What if she lost Rhona too? She had been too busy to pay the slightest attention to Rhona. She had ignored Rhona's problems at school, allowed her no time for questions or conversations, hidden her own feelings. How could she ever hope to be a mother if she couldn't cope with the child already in her care? For a moment all Rhona's grief and torment careered into her own head and the weight of it made her chin and shoulders droop. She stooped over Rhona's bed and asked: 'Where did you get this stuff, sweetheart?'

Rhona just sat up in bed smiling, saying, 'I can't *feel* anything!' with an urgency that contradicted the smirk on her face.

'Well, it's not funny, is it?' Tina looked agitated.

'No, I'm not laughing! I can't get this smile off me! It's just there and I can't get it off! My face hurts – I'm not smiling inside! I want to feel my legs! I just want to be normal again! Help me!'

When Tina drove home it was around four. She called into work and told Keith Pooley why she had not been in that afternoon. Then she went to the Ferabees' to see if Joel was all right, and if he had any ideas about what had happened.

'Well, you'll never guess what!' said Mrs Ferabee. 'He's been sent home from school for drug-dealing! And him only nine year old!' She looked at Joel, who sat red-faced and contrite on the sofa. 'I don't know what's becoming of kids these days. I do not. I never let him watch any videos without seeing what they are and we've never had nothing like this in the family – leastways, not on my side. Not that I'm blaming poor Rhona, mind. She've had a lot to put up with, poor lamb, and it's understandable, what with one thing and whatnot. Well! I've told him, he can forget television from here till Christmas. Course his dad will prob'ly laugh and then we'll be back to square one. Cuppatea?'

While Mrs Ferabee made tea, Tina told Joel that Rhona was in hospital. 'She might be in trouble if they can't find out what she took. Do you know, Joel?'

Joel looked frightened. 'In *hospital*? Like, she might *die* or something?'

'They don't know. You must tell me, Joel. Was it Gabriel?'

Joel shook his head vigorously.

'You do know where she got it from, don't you?'

He nodded slowly. She grabbed his arm and pushed him through the front door ahead of her. 'Show me.'

He took her to a house just two away from her own, in the direction of the open countryside. It stood back from the road, and was entered by an iron gate overgrown with ivy. As she followed Joel down the narrow path, a low whitewashed cottage emerged before them from out of the undergrowth. The door was of heavy oak and studded with black ironwork. She lifted the knocker and let it drop. After a while she peered through the window, but inside it was dark. She turned to Joel. He was biting his lip. Eventually he beckoned her round the side of the house and she tiptoed after him.

There, in a clearing by the back door, a man sat cross-legged, a nose peeking out from two long masses of dull blond hair which skirted the ground in front of him. On the grass was an open tobacco tin full of lumps of brown resin, and a packet of Rizlas. He was fiddling with a paper contraption on the ground, and looked up when he saw the pair arrive.

'Hey!' he said, looking in Tina's direction with eyes that didn't seem to focus on anything in particular. 'Sit down, man!' He hummed to himself, and sprinkled some resin like a stock cube into a long trail of tobacco. 'Just relax – join the party.'

Opposite him, a woman with red hair sat cross-legged in a long patchwork dress, smoking a trumpet-shaped cigarette.

'Bubbles!' breathed Tina in a whispered scream.

Bubbles smiled across at her and carried on beaming, opening and closing her eyelids very slowly.

'Bubbles! What the hell do you think you're doing?'

'Beanie,' said Bubbles, still grinning, all wide-eyed and generous, 'this is Tina.'

'Hey, sit down, man,' said Beanie. 'You're making me nervous. Chill!' He took a drag on the monstrous funnel that Bubbles had handed him, and his head started nodding about in all directions. Tina remained rigid, her mouth ajar, and Joel was fiddling with some cow parsley. 'This woman, right?' His head teetered. 'This woman that you see before you has cured me of a lifetime's malady, right? She is a *green witch*.' He teetered some more and fell backwards, his legs still crossed. 'Hell, man. That stuff's great shit, Bubs!'

Tina was still staring at Bubbles, who was pummelling some substances with a pestle and mortar and humming to herself.

'Bubbles, get up! You're coming home now!' She bent to take her mother-in-law's arm, but Bubbles just stood up serenely.

'Let me show you Beanie's herb garden,' she said, still smiling, and waded into the undergrowth. Tina darted after her, and Joel followed. They walked down a winding path in the back garden, beating back waist-high nettles and brambles, until they came to a well-tended square of tall leafy plants. 'Never seen weed like it,' she sighed, fondling what looked like a tomato plant. 'Look at these buds!'

'Is this what Rhona had?' asked Tina, turning urgently to Joel.

'No. Well, she might of. I don't know what was in those big cigarettes, but she had chocolate cake when we were here.'

'Chocolate cake?'

Joel nodded. Tina glared at Bubbles, who stood surrounded by greenery like a celebrity in *Good Housekeeping*. Her cheeks were full of colour and her deep eyelids drooped sensuously over her green eyes, but her face was a picture of serenity and innocence. 'Beanie makes a good cake,' she said dreamily.

Tina grabbed Joel by the arm and marched him home.

'What happened?' asked Mrs Ferabee. 'You didn't drink your tea.'

Tina apologised and drove to the hospital, leaving them standing at their gate.

'Can't I go with her?' asked Joel.

Mrs Ferabee looked after her as the car drove off. 'It's stewed now.' Then she turned to Joel. 'Tomorrow, perhaps. Anyway, I thought you and Rhona had fallen out.'

'We did, but she loves me now.' He gave a smug sniff. 'It's because I'm a lesbian.'

Sweetheart Red

Gabriel had a dark Celtic look with thick eyebrows and copious hair. As a child he had sat in corners with wax crayons and colouring books, listening but saying nothing. He crawled behind sofas with plastic farm animals and caught crumbs of female conversation. Later he sat chewing gum, slowly picking pieces of Formica off his school desk. Always alone, singled out because of his upbringing and barred from the important gangs. His one ambition was to sort it all out, once and for all, and find the man who could save him. It was for this reason he had tracked Cameron down, after years of research, and come to find him.

Even that, he managed to bodge up. Who else could come face to face with their longed-for father after twenty-four years and, inadvertently, kill him? His sense of gloom and failure was overtaken only by a deep sadness. There was a hole, like a grave, which had never been filled. When he kipped down under the tarpaulin in Tina's shed, he was an open wound. When he woke to find a half-sister, a grandmother and a woman his father loved and knew intimately, he was overwhelmed with fascination. He wanted only to know this family inside out, and to belong at last. But he was cautious. He hadn't planned it this way, of course. But as things stood, he wanted to become indispensable before he revealed himself. Meanwhile, he avoided Rhona's advances as best he could, he warmed with her awe and smarted with her moods; he cherished the smiley stamina of Bubbles, and marvelled at Tina's every move. When he watched her, he could be closer to his father, and when he touched her he could, for a moment, become him.

Now that Tina had blown his cover, he felt the huge cloud of guilt which had descended on him grow thicker and heavier for a while, and then slowly lift. Her angry reaction had given way to something else: a fascination he knew she must feel for the living memento of her lost husband. But now she knew his secrets, he was the more determined to discover hers. He had been watching her. That she might be pregnant was of great import to Gabriel: a new brother or sister. He was aware, despite her best efforts to conceal them, that Tina brought home items of babywear and smuggled them into drawers and cupboards. He could not help noticing – when he emptied the bins – screwed up Mothercare bags and discarded sleepsuit tags. The more he suspected, the more closely he watched her, certain she would give herself away openly soon.

He noticed she often slipped out for a walk in the early evening on Fridays. He had followed her on the last two occasions and had seen her disappear into the churchyard. Today she returned late after phoning from the hospital and asking him to get Bubbles home. The sun was beginning to set now, but she changed from her overalls and went to pick flowers at the back of the house. He knew what she was visiting, and he wanted to grieve there too.

He followed at a distance; down the road, across it, and in through the wooden gate. She crouched by the grave, and he watched from behind the church porch as she removed some flowers and arranged the new ones, took them out again and doggedly rearranged each one. Then he saw the back of her dress swinging down the path, heard the sob of the gate as it swung to.

The gravestone was small and of whitish stone. He approached it nervously. It read:

Rory Edward Morrison
April 20th 1994 – July 11th 1994
We will always love you

Underneath was carved:

I will lend thee for a little time
A child of mine, said GOD

'said GOD' appeared to have been added later, as if the stonemason had felt the need to attribute the quotation.

He squatted and fell forward on to his knees. He felt the ground with his hand, warm in the sun, and kneaded the grass until his knuckles burned.

'Is this the junkies' ward?' said Keith Pooley, peeking through a curtain around Rhona's bed and smiling. 'Feeling any better?'

Rhona did feel better. It was Saturday morning. She felt as though her limbs were thawing out, and she gave him a watery smile which she governed herself. He stroked her hair and she rested her cheek on his hand. They remained in silence for several minutes, each choking a little on words which wouldn't come out. Eventually Rhona looked up at him and said, 'No one likes me.'

He pulled a giant bear from a carrier bag and some pop magazines. 'I think you're smashing.'

She smiled again and a tear rolled quickly down one cheek, and then the other. 'I only did it to be liked.'

'I know.'

'Now nobody'll speak to me. No one's *allowed* to speak to me now. I just messed up big time.'

He looked thoughtful. 'Is there anything I can do for you, sweetheart?'

She sat up on one elbow and began to look conspiratorial. 'There is, actually. I made another big mistake and now I don't think I can undo it. Mum's dating all these men and it's my fault. It was my idea and now I think it stinks. I only wanted a man to do our house up, but these complete morons keep coming round and messing our lives up. And the latest one is horrible.'

'I can't do much about that.' But he felt suddenly very protective of Tina.

'You might be able to, actually. You see I know where they're going on Wednesday, and on Thursday, after her therapy meeting.'

'Therapy?'

'Yeah. He's her therapist and he came on to her, and I know she hates him. She just can't shake him off. He's *molesting* her. I was thinking, if you could just go and save her from him—'

'Are you sure she wants to be saved?'

Rhona reached over, put her arms round his neck and kissed him. 'Of course! It's you she wants. We both do!'

Keith felt light-headed as he walked down the hospital corridor. The tiled floor seemed to have turned into a trampoline, or a moving path like the ones at airports. Each stride seemed to take him further than ever before, and he thought he might take off.

When he rounded the corner into the foyer, he almost bumped into Tina going the other way. She smiled and said it was 'sweet' of him to visit Rhona, and thanked him. He sailed on by, feeling sweet and alluring, when a thought struck him. He might just go and check up with Tina – find out if this bloke really was bothering her. He didn't want to be an unwelcome hero, and it might all be wishful thinking on Rhona's part.

He turned and went back up the corridor, and entering the ward he heard Tina and Rhona speaking from behind the curtains.

'I'm sorry, Mum.'

'No, *I'm* sorry. I haven't been spending enough time with you. I should've—'

'You're always thinking of me. It's just that no one likes me. Look at the party, you spent ages—'

'No, no, no! I screwed everything up. The reason no one came was because I invited children from the wrong *school*, for heaven's sake.'

'Not all of them, though. Some rang up, didn't they, to say they couldn't come?'

'Well . . . I left it all to the last minute. Parents need to plan things.'

There was a silence. Keith thought now would be a good time to make his presence known, but then he heard Rhona sobbing.

'You're going to leave me and I don't blame you! Rory was your real baby – I'm just a burden to you!'

'Don't be daft!'

'Dad was right. He said you do everything for me and I'm not grateful.'

'I'll let you into a little secret about parents,' he heard Tina say. 'They may do everything for you, but what they don't tell you is that it's a *pleasure* to do everything for you. An indescribable pleasure.'

Keith rocked forward on his feet, and then back again. Little stars were gathering round the edge of his vision and blanking out everything except a flower in the curtain. Tina had had a *baby*?

'You teach us so much, you see. We learn lots from you—'

There was a muffled silence. Keith stood very still.

'You're crying,' said Rhona.

'No, I'm not.'

He would have liked to see it too; just peek round the curtains, perhaps. But he felt completely stuck. Eventually he tiptoed to the vending machine in the corridor and bought a KitKat. He couldn't eat it, and it melted in his pocket on the way home.

Tina lay in bed, wakeful. A passing car made a spotlight on the ceiling, and dipped across the room. She felt renewed in some way: by the revelations about Cameron, Gabriel's identity, her tenderness towards Rhona. And there was something else. She realised she was looking forward to the next day – and the next. Carl's face appeared in every thought, and she let him flood her head. She drifted on a pond in a low boat, her hand rippling the surface of the water, and looked up to see his keyboard teeth as he rowed her in the sunshine. They checked into hotels in tropical countries and had rolls for breakfast. She turned over on a sunbed and saw him peering up from something clever and psychological and saying, 'Hmmm.' They crossed country stiles in Aran knits and floated through tuneful winter wonderlands in matching mittens. She glided up the aisle in a cloud of white organza towards his welcoming gaze. He kissed her neck as she sat at an imaginary dressing table with triple mirrors. She strolled on his arm in Mothercare and flipped truckloads of babygrows on the counter, saying, 'Next week!' They sent cards to friends at Christmas and signed them 'Carl, Tina (and Bump!!)'. She didn't hear the milk float at four o'clock.

Honeybee Yellow

TEST FOR DAMP: to discover whether damp is striking through or resulting from condensation inside, make a square wall of plasticine or Blu-tack and cover with a glass tile. Tina sat on the floor of the bedroom reading one of Keith's manuals. *Press to within 3mm of the wall. Leave for three days during a period when damp patches form. If droplets form on the underside of the glass, damp is striking through. If droplets form on the surface of the glass, you have condensation.*

Plasticine reminded her of babies' fingers. She went to the adjoining room, rummaged in a drawer and opened a tube of nappy cream. She sat sniffing until the sniffs turned to sobs. Smells were the cruellest of all.

Inside her memories she could still see the jittery head teetering on narrow shoulders, coming to rest in the crook of her arm. The nape of his neck had smelt of vanilla, and his temples of baked potatoes. She could still stroke the hands, feel their softness and the dimple at the base of each finger. They were strong and damp, and when he was asleep the fingers were like little sausages of warm plasticine.

When Rory was born the reedy legs dangled from his body as thin as chicken bones. At eleven weeks, though, the plump flesh on each inner thigh was furrowed by two horizontal cherub folds. He was growing every day, blooming full and pink, unstoppable. And then one morning at four o'clock she found him limp and cold as snow. She picked him up and he flopped like a rag doll.

She watched that moment over and over like a video you could replay, pause, rewind, and play again. Her heart had beaten so fast she couldn't tell if it was her pulse or his. The head fell back limply and she pushed her mouth to his, covering the nose as well. She breathed all her life into him. Then Cameron was there, taking the baby from her and wrapping him in a cellular blanket. She let out a howl like a she wolf, an unending lament that screamed through the partition walls down the terrace. She shocked herself with its volume. It reminded her of a birthing howl, but this one spoke of a wound that would never heal. It broke all barriers. She was a quiet no-fuss person who didn't flinch at pain or shout in anger. But everyone, she thought, had one howl in them. This had been hers.

This week she would have to talk about it all at the therapy group, and knew it was impossible. She had neglected Rhona; she could say that. She knew she must stop reliving the past before she swallowed up what was left of the present in bitter regret. And it wasn't Cameron's fault: that was a good start. She loved him – she had always loved him. He couldn't be held responsible for all that had led up to their baby's death, and all that had gone before in her own life. It was just so painful to think that Rory might, *might* have lived if only a whole set of circumstances had been ever so slightly different. If, for example, Cameron hadn't been worried about money, he might have been able to sleep better, and the baby wouldn't have been sleeping in a different room.

'It's time that baby stopped sleeping in our bed!' she heard him say, over and over in her head. 'Let him sleep in the cot! That's what we paid good money for, isn't it? A cot, you said, we have to have a proper cot. Well, put him *in* it! He's five weeks old!' So she had tucked Rory up by the side of their bed in his second-hand cot with painted bears at the head and base. She would prop herself up on her elbow several times each night, trying not to rustle their bedclothes, and place a hand on Rory's tummy. She waited for the gentle rise and fall, then sank back under the sheets to Cameron's heavy sigh. And when she lifted the baby out to feed him, Cameron would roll over heavily and hunch his back at her, as though this were some uncalled-for night-time pleasure she was according herself.

Not once did he change a nappy or hold Rory for a moment after he started crying – except when friends came to see him. Then he would hold the baby up to the ceiling, making affectionate cooing noises close to his face, and change a nappy with a great flourish of expertise.

Then at ten weeks he said: 'Can't you put that baby in his own room? We have *got* a baby room, remember? I only spent all Easter doing it up!' She had transferred him meekly to the boxroom, with its Honeybee Yellow wallpaper and giraffe borders. They couldn't afford a baby transmitter, Cameron said, so she spent the first three nights on the floor by the cot, listening to the sound of Rory's breath and nestling him next to her after his feeds. She could remember the surprise of her breasts: swollen, rounded and pale in the fuzzy night light, new parts of her that dictated the pattern of day and night. She could see his little head now, rocking to the side in search of her nipple in the dark. Always finding it, like a small animal that knows instinctively where it needs to be.

It wasn't Cameron's fault that she left the baby to sleep in his own room – it had to happen sooner or later. It was just . . . if only . . . Rory had a cold, she thought. She had wanted to sleep in the boxroom that night and Cameron had sighed one of those sighs. 'For God's sake, Tina! He's got to sleep on his own *some* time!' And it wasn't as if it were that night it happened, but the night after, when she had begun to relax a little.

But he had *promised*. If she could just stick it out for two more years . . . or three . . . She had held her own dead baby in her arms and listened to him say, 'We'll have another,' as if he could pop down to the pet shop and replace it like a run-over kitten. What he meant was it might be all for the best, really. They could plan the next one for a more economically appropriate moment.

Tina went back to the bedroom and sank beside the DIY manual. His death could only be another punishment for what she did with Dermot. There was no other explanation, and she liked things to be explained neatly, otherwise they joined a mass of unknown things which seemed to chain her down.

Look for other clues too. Warm wet weather would suggest damp striking through; but if patches occur in cold weather it is almost certainly an internal problem.

It was early Tuesday evening, two days before the therapy group, and Gabriel was giving Tina some of his advice in the kitchen.

'All you need to worry about,' he said, wagging a finger at her, 'is (a) can he afford to take on all your debts? and (b) will he make a good father to Rhona?'

'A good sperm count might be more to the point,' said Tina, wishing she hadn't told Gabriel about the encounter, but anxious to talk about Carl to someone.

'Oh, I *see*!' So she wasn't expecting Cameron's baby after all. He threw an orange in the air and caught it in his open hand. He stared at the orange for a while, and thought. He would have to act quickly. 'Hey look, Tina,' he said, 'I've got a brilliant idea, right?'

'What?'

'Sit down.' He folded her into a chair and sat opposite her. 'Seriously now, I've got a proposition to make, right, and I want you to think about it very carefully before you say no.'

'Fire away.'

'Well, you're like nervous about all this dating stuff, right? You want a baby, but you're not sure if you want a husband, right?'

'I didn't say that.'

'Well, the thing is, you want *Cameron's* baby.'

Tina frowned and looked at a pattern in the linoleum.

'OK,' he said, lifting his hands as if in defence, 'now don't say anything, but . . . well . . . I could father your child – and it would have Cameron's genes!'

Tina threw her head back and smiled wryly. 'Thanks for the offer, Gabe.' She breathed out a laugh of disbelief. 'You're my husband's *son*, for goodness' sake. I think I'll give it a miss.'

'No – you don't understand! Obviously it would be better to . . . to . . . to sleep together . . . sort of thing, but I'd be prepared – if you thought it really necessary – to follow my father's example and . . . what I'm saying is . . . I'd be prepared to donate sperm.'

Tina stared at him.

'Obviously if it didn't work after a while, we could move on to . . . on to the real thing, as it were.'

Tina laughed then, but disappeared to change into a dress and went out for a walk to think.

It was a quarter past six. She was walking down Lambpen Lane beyond the church and thought she might collect some flowers for the grave. She wore a loose buttercup print and felt weightless after hours of heavy overalls. The hedgerows on either side rose up steeply, blooming thick with dog roses, celandines, nettles and long tubes of honeysuckle. Buried in a cloud of foliage was a kissing-gate which creaked on rusty hinges as she pushed it. She was about to fold the gate back on itself so that she could pass into the field, when a figure appeared in front of her from behind the hedge. She looked up, startled. About two feet away stood a masked man. A faded checked shirt was open to the waist, and revealed a deep matt tan with a path of dark velvet hair leading towards the belly and disappearing into soft denim. The chest was heaving gently and she could feel the warmth rise from it like steam from where he stood. She breathed in a resiny smell and could feel her heart-rate quickening: she looked at the mask in alarm. It said nothing. Her hand began to tremble on the gate.

'What do you want?' she said at last.

The mask said something she could barely make out, and a hand went up to raise the wire mesh visor. 'I'm sorry, I forgot you can't see me in this,' said Keith Pooley. 'Kept it on 'cos the sun was in my eyes.' He signalled to the visor: 'For the bees.'

She closed her eyelids.

'Hope I didn't surprise you!'

He had surprised her. She was speechless. He creaked the gate open from his side and they stood in the semicircular pen together for a moment, aware they had betrayed the purpose of the gate, until he exited into the lane.

Gooseberry Fool

Keith Pooley bathed when he got home. He put on a smart suit and then took it off again. He tried a casual beige jacket, but removed it. He walked up and down his bedroom in jeans and a T-shirt. 'Hey, you!' he said, looking in the mirror. 'Can't you see when you're not wanted?' Then he took it all off and put on a clean Did-It-Myself outfit. He ruffled his curly hair and flexed his biceps to his reflection, and in a deep, liquidy voice he said, 'Move over, mister.'

The cocktail bar was fairly quiet when he arrived, and he could see they weren't there. He crossed to the other side of the road and took a newspaper from the top of a waste bin. Then he leant against the wall of the Midland Bank and pretended to read it, unaware that his eyes peeped out above the naked body of a page three girl whose gigantic breasts gleamed like beacons down the entire street.

As he waited, he remembered his last meeting with Linda in the restaurant. 'It's ten thousand pounds a year, and we thought you might help out, seeing's you've had nothing to pay for donkeys' years.' This was what she had crossed the Atlantic to tell him: that his daughter had her heart set on stage school in London, and if he wanted to see her again he could. The catch was money. Keith was sickened by his position. Carol had been worked up to believe that her ambitions could be fulfilled in London, and that her father would pay. Any refusal now turned him into a dastardly villain. But 'Steady on, Lin, I barely *earn* that much, after tax' was met with statements that he had had an easy time of it financially, not having had to look after Carol. 'But I *would* of! I would've given her anything!'

'Well, now's your chance!'

There had been hollows forming in his stomach, filling with broken sentences and jumbled words. He knew he had something important to say – something which would vindicate him and clamp Linda's smudge-proof mouth shut for ever – but he couldn't find it in the messed up drawer of thoughts. He felt he had been cheated out of Carol's upbringing, but his anger and disappointment were more like a hunger. There was something he couldn't quite put his finger on; he could sense it, just out of reach. Suddenly he was standing on the balls of his feet again, listening to Tina from behind the hospital curtain.

It had been an education for him when Carol was small, and when she was wrenched away he was like a boy with a brilliant career ahead of him who'd been condemned to finish his days in the dole queue. Being free to give to Carol had been the most liberating and exhilarating feeling of his life. She took all, rejecting nothing, treasured his kisses, begged for more stories. He had been set free to love, and the more he gave, the more he felt. Some days he felt he was fit to burst with it all, and she just kept on smiling and cuddling and asking for more. He built her slides in the garden out of softwood, and a pond with stone ducks from Garden Accessories. He made her kites from balsa wood, a doll's house, a hamster run, a sandpit, a cot. He grew her fresh vegetables, sang her to sleep and told her stories about bears. He changed her nappies, emptied her potties, dabbed her scuffed knees with TCP. When she was ill everything else came to a standstill, and the rest of the world became unfocused and blurred when her peachy cheeks were folded into dimples by a smile. Giving to her had been part of his growing. When she was snatched away he felt stunted. Tina was right.

'All that giving,' he told Linda, 'it does you good.' Linda had been pleased, and snapped her handbag shut to go. Then she was confused that he didn't write her a cheque.

After fifteen minutes, Tina and Carl appeared around the corner arm in arm and smiling. You had to give it to her: she looked stunning. Someone should tell her, though, that this was not the way to get rid of a man. She wore a blue print dress with matching shoes, and her hair was loose. He could no longer see her face, as it was tilted up to the side, looking at Carl as he spoke. He seemed to be doing all the talking.

Keith waited five minutes and then crossed the road. He could see Clint push open the saloon bar doors and touch his hat, and he began to slow his pace as he reached the opposite pavement. Pace was everything. He gave the glass door a smart shove, and it didn't budge. He pushed a little harder, and still it remained closed. He put his shoulder to it, and two girls came out of the adjacent door, giggling, pushing it open from the inside. He could see Tina at a corner table as he swung into the smoky bar, her face still turned to Carl's, obviously bored to death. Keith adjusted his collar, cleared his throat, and walked slowly over to them. Carl looked up, but Tina didn't notice at first. Keith took the back of a chair and swung it next to hers. 'Mind if I siddown?'

Now she was looking up and awestruck. Her eyebrows shot up and she blinked. She breathed out heavily. (Relief?)

'Do I know you?' asked Carl.

'Do now,' said Keith, his hand going up to touch his hat, and then remembering he didn't have one. 'Mind if I join you?'

'What the—' started Tina.

'Can I help you?' asked the waitress.

Keith took one look at the cocktail list and read out the first thing he saw. 'I'll have a long slow screw against the wall,' he said, raising an eyebrow and then lowering it swiftly. Best be stony.

'You like those, do you?' said Carl sardonically.

'Ask her.' Keith nodded towards Tina. 'She should know.'

Tina's jaw dropped open like a puppet's. 'What the—'

'Do you two know each other?' asked Carl.

'She's my wife,' said Keith, at exactly the same time as Tina said, 'I've never met him before.' There was a brief silence, and Tina said, 'He's my employer,' at the very moment Keith said, 'Well, my lover.'

Carl looked from one to the other. Keith looked at Tina and said, 'Don't you think you'd better stop this nonsense and come home now?'

'*Home?* With *you*?'

Keith winked. 'The kids are waiting.' He motioned his head towards the door and winked again excessively. 'You know – the *kids*.'

'The kids,' said Tina, puzzled. And then more panicked: 'Is Rhona OK?'

'She's fine—'

'Bubbles? She's escaped!'

'No, no.'

'*Bubbles?*' said Carl to Tina.

'Then *what*?' said Tina to Keith.

Keith put his arm round her in desperation. 'I want you home with me. Come on, now.' He winked again and started to pull her to her feet, but she pushed him away violently.

'Get away from me! Leave me alone! I don't know what's got into you, Keith Pooley. The only time in my life ever something good happens to me and *you* have to come and bugger it up for me! Just sod off and leave me alone!'

She was standing up now, recoiling from him as if he were infected.

'But I thought—'

'Just bugger off!'

He seemed to shrink several inches in height, and could feel his toes sweating. The whole surface of his skin prickled with discomfort, and he turned to leave, colliding with the waitress who spilt his Long Slow Screw over his Did-It-Myself sleeve and the floor. He couldn't think what to do now. He wasn't sure this ever happened to Clint.

Carl picked up the tabloid paper that Keith had left folded on the table, and held it out away from him with fingers like pincers. 'Who let *him* in?' He dropped the two giant breasts on to the tiled floor. 'Is that really your employer?'

Her nostrils twitched and she was conscious of people looking in their direction. She watched the floor as cocktail seeped in across the naked woman's pink bosom, up across her neck and face, turning a darker pink. Who would have believed it? She had thought better of Keith Pooley. 'Will you walk me home?'

She invited him in for a coffee, nervously surveying the kitchen for anything it might say about her. But the washing up was done and the table was free of crumbs. Rhona was sitting at it watchfully with a crayon and paper. As Tina filled the kettle, Carl asked Rhona what she was drawing. She looked up archly and showed him her dress design. 'It's an office dress,' she said, explaining the miniature phone on the shoulder, the belt full of pens like a bullet belt, the matching pink notepads on each cuff, the tiny coffee cups hidden in the heel of each shoe, and the handbag made of chocolate in case you were too busy to eat properly.

'Wouldn't the chocolate melt?' he asked.

Rhona tilted her head to one side and looked at her design. Then she put her head down in a hurt retreat, and covered it from his view with her arm.

He smiled as Tina gave him his coffee. 'Any sugar?'

Gabriel pounded down the stairs and into the room, and plonked a jar on the table between their two mugs.

'There you go!' He looked pleased with himself. 'Mission accomplished!'

'What's that?' asked Carl.

'Sperm – double load!'

Carl scratched his nose and said he had better give the coffee a miss after all – he just remembered something. He would call her.

Plum Crush

The following day was Thursday, and Tina had failed to show up to work. Keith Pooley knew he would have to go round after his shift to apologise. At ten past six he arrived home and ran a bath. He removed his clothes and stood in front of the steaming bathroom cabinet mirror, trying out a few faces. 'I'm *so* sorry, Tina.' He cleared his throat. 'Tina, I know you'll never forgive me, but let me explain.' Perhaps she wouldn't even let him through the door. 'I have some important news – may I come in?' What would Clint say? He raised an eyebrow trying to achieve the right blend of intrigue and regret. Then he raised both, and tilted his head to one side. He saw a brown, leathery face with white lines forking out dramatically from the edge of his eyes where he had squinted at the sun in his allotment. His pale neck looked so long he felt that if he looked down he might find his head was on a stick, like one of those novelties at the end of a pencil. His ears grew so large and red that they filled the entire bathroom and started to flap, bearing him through the ceiling and far off across the fields. The steam was closing in and covered the last chink of mirror. It was no use. *He* wouldn't invite him in, in her shoes.

It was Rhona who answered the door. She looked embarrassed. 'Come in. Are you angry with me?'

'Course not. I should've known better. I made a fool of myself.'

'No you didn't. You did the right thing, only she doesn't know it yet.' She lowered her voice to a whisper: 'If he's such a great bloke, why is he a rapist?' She looked over her shoulder to check that no one was coming and handed him a card solemnly. Keith looked at the frenetic handwriting: *Ca rl Sal ter: The rapist.*

'Therapist,' he said. 'He's not a rapist. He's what she wants and I've ruined it for her.' He watched Rhona frown, sulkily. 'Is she in?'

'I'll go and get her. She's trying on dresses – she's been *hours* already.'

He could hear Bubbles singing loudly in her annexe:

> ' . . . She said Young man dissemble,
> My company forsake
> For it's to my good opinion
> I fear you are some rake . . .'

No sooner had Rhona left the kitchen than the phone rang in the corner. Keith looked at it and wondered if he should pick it up. It stopped ringing and there was a click, followed by a long bleep: 'I'm sorry, we can't come to the phone at the moment,' said a male voice, 'but please leave a message after the tone.'

He knew this must be Cameron, and felt quite knocked backwards by the sound of a dead man speaking. It was a wonder she hadn't changed it, but then, he supposed he wouldn't either, if he lost a wife. His thoughts were halted by another long bleep and the sound of another man's voice: *Tina? It's Carl. You there? OK. I'm sorry I won't be able to see you after the session tonight, but my father's been taken ill and I need to go and see him in hospital. I'll be running the session as usual, so I'll hope to see you there at seven thirty. Perhaps we can have dinner tomorrow instead. Byee!*

Keith frowned and felt awkward, but just as he began to feel relief that it was over and he need no longer feel like an eavesdropper, something extraordinary happened.

Happy now? said Carl on the phone.

Keith opened his mouth to answer.

I told you, you'll have a much better time at this party, came another man's voice, *so don't say you're doing it for* me. *Mind you, she's probably all dolled up to go out now.*

Oh, don't worry about her. *She's not really my type – got a bit of a fat arse. Very sweet and all that, but far too* clingy. *She hangs on my every word. Bit dim, too. And she's so desperate to get married and have kids.*

Poor cow— The voice trailed off and there were some felty sounds in the background for a while.

So why're you still seeing her?

She's tongue out for it! A dead cert.

Well, there'll be plenty of chicks there tonight, don't you— There was a dull 'thlunk' and the tape came to an end.

Keith felt as though someone had rotated him several times. He had a bitter taste in his mouth and his head was thudding. He couldn't let Tina hear that about herself. He went over to the answer phone and hovered over the eject button. He had no right to remove her messages. And wouldn't she be hurt anyway if she went on seeing this animal? But then, this bloke would probably be more tactful if he finished with her face to face. It would be a private hurt, not a public humiliation. But then again, what if he seduced her like he said? And what if she heard the message and knew that he had overheard it? Or maybe the whole household would hear it, or maybe she would play it back in front of a friend. It was too harsh. He couldn't bear for her to be hurt.

He could hear footsteps on the stairs and Rhona saying: 'But you look tarty in that one – the blue's far better.' His fingers felt heavy and he could hardly move them. He pressed the eject button and flipped out the tape. Perhaps he could erase just the awful bit and come back to replace it while Tina was out.

'Oh,' said Tina. 'It's you.'

Keith looked startled, fumbling with the tape in his trouser pocket. 'Yes.'

Tina was fiddling with the contents of her handbag, and looked up questioningly. But he said nothing. He felt that all words had temporarily been beaten out of him with a carpet beater. He watched the back of her neck as she looked into a compact mirror and folded her lips together. The kitchen was tatty and there was a greasy pot of spaghetti on the oilclothed table, rust marks on the fridge and cracked soap at the sink which was marbled with dirt. But in that one corner of the kitchen where she stood was a pocket of elegance, a cloud of femininity that smelt of flowers and spices and made him dizzy. He opened his mouth and breathed heavily, and Tina snapped her bag shut. 'Well, I'm off. Rhona has to go to bed at nine, so don't chat to her for too long. Gabe's babysitting.'

'. . . Then dark she followed him,
His teeth so bright did shine,
And he led her over the mountain
That sly bold Reynardine.'

She knew she was early, but wanted to speak to him alone before the rest of the group arrived. The College of Further Education was lit in only two corners of its sprawling campus. She went down an echoing corridor filled with artwork and stopped in front of the old swing doors where the bereavement class was held. She could hear voices, and didn't want to interrupt any class that hadn't finished. Then the voices stopped. She peeked in through a small window near the top of the door and saw two people kissing. One of them was Carl, and the other was a woman she recognised from the week before who had lost her poodle in a road accident. She frowned as if her eyes must be lying to her. Then she leant against the wall with her head and arms like a flying buttress and felt her throat constricting. After a minute she noticed a sign inches from her eyes: 'STILL LIFE' and decided that there was. Harry, a pensioner from the previous week who'd lost his wife, came careering down the corridor with his walking stick. 'Hello there, Tina! Coming in?'

She followed him into a room which was cold and badly decorated. In one corner the pale green paint bubbled from the walls over a mass of damp. In another, Carl sat serenely, nodding and smiling as people came in.

Despite her state of mind – or because of it – Tina was moved by the accounts of each member of the group. One or two of them made tears spill down her cheek and she wiped them away when no one was looking. Harry had lost his wife after sixty years of marriage and five years of nursing her. A man with a stutter called Raymond had lost his mother as a child and hadn't mourned her properly. A teenaged girl with no eyebrows had lost her boyfriend in a motorbike accident. Carl's kissing partner kept bashfully quiet most of the time. They listened to each other and asked questions. Tina found it soothing, although she said nothing of another grief – still unmourned.

Carl had a way of waiting several moments after each person

had spoken before saying anything, as if this silence enhanced his words of great wisdom. Not that he offered advice as such: he only ever asked questions that seemed to make you feel instructed.

'What would you like to say to Cameron, Tina, if he were here now?' He waited a long, pompous time and she said nothing. 'Wouldn't you like to say you're . . . *angry*, maybe?' She stared at a patch in the linoleum that looked like Australia. 'Wouldn't you like to take this cushion – here – and imagine it's Cameron?' He handed her a limp mustard-coloured cushion filled with feathers and went to sit down again. 'Don't you want to punch him, Tina? You do, don't you? He's left you in this mess without even a goodbye. He's left you with debts you can't pay and responsibilities that should be shared – go on! Show your anger!'

Tina felt foolish. She looked at a peak of velvet at the corner of the cushion and dented it sheepishly with her fist.

'Come on, Tina! Go for it! He's left you up shit creek and you're *angry*! Go on, thump him!'

Tina stood up, dropped the cushion on the chair and made for the door, crying. He ran after her and grabbed her sleeve. 'Come on, Tina! Let it *out*! You need to give vent to all that pent-up rage!' She began punching his chest and kicking his shins. Harry shouted, 'Yeah! Go for it!' and Carl said, 'Good girl! That's it! You're *angry*! Let it all *out*!'

She pulled her fist back and punched him full on the nose.

Harry stopped cheering and the room fell silent. At any rate, she could hear nothing but a distant ringing in her ears. Carl's body sank to the ground like a beanbag, and seemed to grow smaller as he slumped into a little heap on the linoleum. His face was covered in blood and it seemed impossible that she could have produced this scene herself. Her knuckles were killing her. She stood for a while, breathing heavily and observing the poodle girl rush over with a Wet-One from her handbag. Then she pushed open the swing door with her elbow and went home to do some plastering.

Texas Rose

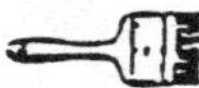

This is what Keith Pooley did on Thursday evenings: he shaved for a second time in the day and had a soak in a scented bath. He listened to the radio, and when the programme changed he got out, padded over to the airing cupboard and took out a large warm towel. He sprinkled his feet with medicated talcum powder and sometimes he would sing to an imaginary microphone, or mime the songs on the radio. Then he would go into the bedroom and put on a fresh shirt, jeans and cowboy boots. He wore a small metal plaque at his neck with two black thongs descending from it, and before he went out he packed his wallet with crisp new notes, put on a stetson and said 'Howdy!' to the mirror.

He drove – or walked if it was summer – along Church Road and into Moorhampton Road, which meandered into town. In the Polish Club hall, above a Greek takeaway, was the weekly country and western night. On this particular Thursday he had already bathed to go and apologise to Tina, and his dressing routine was a little broken. And on this particular Thursday he was going to take a lady guest, although he didn't know as much when he set out.

When Tina came home all red-faced and caught him and Rhona fiddling with the answerphone he said, 'I'm late,' and then, 'Well, I'll be off,' and saw that it was not the right thing to say at all. She didn't rush upstairs or run away; she sat square in a kitchen chair and blubbered. Rhona went to put her arm round her, but she only lifted her head and spluttered, 'Why aren't you in bed?'

'It's only a quarter to eight!' But Rhona made to leave the room anyway, and stood in the doorway behind her stepmother, grimacing at Keith as if to say, 'Go on! Get in there!'

Keith fidgeted and fiddled with his neck thongs. 'Hey, now. What on earth's happened?'

More sobs.

'Someone been upsetting you?'

Wails.

'Being nasty, and that?'

No response.

'Or maybe you just come over all sad about what's happened. Hits some people like that, they reckon. One minute they act so's butter wouldn't melt in their mouth, next thing you know some little thing sets them off and they cry out months of pain, for example, that they ought to of got rid of earlier, maybe.'

She sniffed and frowned and looked at him. Her eyes seemed greener, set off by a network of contrasting red capillaries. He could see that she was covered in tears, and her top lip was wet from nose-running. He felt awkward about seeing her so dicey. She was so organised and competent, and now here she was all raw and precarious. He felt as though he were trying to walk on one leg and might topple over at any moment and lose the opportunity for good, or else there might be no opportunity at all. Something was expected of him and he didn't know what. He only knew that what he did next was crucial. He was so nervous at the prospect that his mind suddenly went blank. He reached out instinctively and put his arm round her.

'There, there,' he said. 'You look a real knock-out in that dress.'

She breathed out, 'Well, I won't be going anywhere in it,' and she put her head down on the table and disappeared from sight.

'Well, that's a bit of a shame. You looking so lovely and all that. Now, I suggest you don't waste it.'

So he invited her, and after a minute she raised her blotchy face and said, 'Yes. Why not?'

The hall smelt of polish, and photographs and trophies of the various groups that used it lined the walls: Brownies, aerobic classes, Freemasons and T'ai Chi. As they sat at one of the small round tables along the side, Tina felt calmer and pleased to be occupied, but her insides still churned and she didn't really care where she was. They sipped at bottled beers and watched a local band playing numbers that Keith recognised and tapped his foot to. People kept stopping on their way to the bar to greet him. He seemed to know everyone: a man with very white teeth and a lassoo congratulated him on his acacia honey; a couple with matching red gingham in their outfits said, 'Hi, Keith!'; a plump woman with a cummerbund and purple feathers smiled, 'How you doin'?'; and two identical men with beer froth on their moustaches slapped his shoulder. He introduced her to all of them as 'My good friend, Tina' and everywhere she looked were smiling faces.

After a while the MC called people up for a dance, and women seemed to appear from the shadows in colourful dirndls and puffed sleeves, accompanied by men with kerchiefs, waistcoats and heeled boots. Then the polished wooden floor sprang up and down to fiddle, banjo and electric guitar. In front of their table Tina could see the close-up of a back – which changed with each few bars – and the laughing heads of couples bobbing up and down under arm arches or swinging round and round like little wooden figures predicting sunshine. Hands were clapping and feet were stamping. Keith Pooley kept up a gentle tap with his right boot and her eyes went down to it, examining his outfit on the way. Then the tune changed subtly, there was applause and a murmur, and the MC urged them to stay on the floor for the next number. The beer bottles started to jig up and down and people squeezed past with trayloads of drinks, skirting the dancers and laughing if they knocked into them.

After the dancing, a girl – introduced as 'Peggy-Lou-Anne' ('Her real name's Sharon Pincher,' whispered Keith) – wove her way through a few people and across the stage holding a microphone very close to her lips and giving out a strong, tuneful whine. She wore a dress of red and yellow check, the small squares over her bosom turning into lozenges and triangles where darts pinched the material into her tiny waist. She looked little more than thirteen and sang, 'I cried all the way to the altar.'

Tina was impressed by her sureness. 'I didn't know you were into country and western,' she said.

He leant closer in order to hear her. 'Ah, well. There's a lot about me you don't know, I 'spect.' Then the two men with moustaches got up to sing 'Two Little Orphans'.

At nine thirty a man in a dark uniform went up to the stage and blew a bugle. There was a sudden hush. After the last clink of glass everyone stood solemnly in total silence and the lights were lowered. Tina was awestruck as an army of men – some in uniform – marched in single file from the men's cloakroom and came to rest in rows behind a flag-bearer. Then a fife and drum started up and she felt a chill of fear. Another file of soldiers marched in from between the bar and the soft drinks machine. All she could make out in the dark were shadowy figures with hats and silver buttons, and two flag-bearers facing each other. The drum pattered menacingly, and she leant towards Keith for an explanation. He put his hand to her ear and, careful not to make any sound which would disturb the ceremony, he whispered, 'It's the North versus the South – Civil War and that.'

Suddenly, a figure from one side held up a white flag and asked for hostilities to cease for the length of the evening. A spokesman for the other side agreed, in a lengthy speech, and the lights came on as they all filed out again to people clapping and cheering. Tina sighed with relief, but Keith was on his feet and pullling her up by the hand. 'Come on – let's dance!

'But I can't!'

'I'll show you.'

He whisked her on to the dance floor and the band started to play something catchy. He pushed her away with his right hand and pulled her back in again, smelling of soap. She moved like a rag doll: 'But I really *can't*!' she whined. He just smiled and span her round. To her surprise, she ended up facing him again, and he took her waist and did a few steps to the right and the left. Then he polka'd with her around the side of the room, and she was amazed to see that her feet were doing the same as everyone else's. She looked up at him and saw a brilliant white shirt with matching teeth. His waist, when she took it, felt more solid than she had expected. His hold on her was more purposeful than she might have imagined, although not too tight. He seemed to know what he was doing and he made her glide. It was exhilarating to be whirled away and then to connect so beautifully. She belonged to a pattern. They floated and drifted and then knit back together again. She was buoyant, airborne. They looped the loop, they skimmed the rooftops. They went into orbit.

At last the music stopped. Everyone was clapping, and she was applauding as loud as anyone, catching her breath and laughing, when the MC announced the next singer: 'Our very own Keith – the Kid – Pooley!' Tina slowed her sweaty clapping and noticed that he was gone. She stared at the stage.

A tall imposing figure strode over to the microphone, the slow click of the metal boot studs indicating a body mass not to be tampered with. He lifted the microphone from its stand and looked at the floor. The electric guitar twanged into a melancholy introduction, and he tilted his head back and sang, without any effort at all.

People had returned to their seats or to lean on the bar, and a few couples swayed in the centre of the hall. Tina stood where he had left her, gaping at the crooning cowboy who moved so easily across the stage:

'Ain't gonna take the road no more
I've searched the world Lord knows,
But I found you right outside my door
My darlin' Texas Rose . . .'

She was perfectly sober, yet everything around her seemed dream-like. She proceeded in a slow, uneven path towards her chair, as if the whole hall were rocking like a boat. But before she could sit down he sang:

'So take that chair by my chair
Where the homely fire glows
And we could sit together there
For ever, Texas Rose . . .'

She looked up, startled, but no one was looking at her. All eyes were on Keith, except for the slow couples who rocked in each other's arms in front of the stage. At last she sat down, and imagined that he must have sung this song many times before – since Linda left him, perhaps. Even so, she was in shock, and she supposed it was a mixture of having hit a man on the nose just hours beforehand, and her surprise at Keith's versatility and grace. He had a presence she hadn't expected, and she felt something very strongly for the first time in months: that she was not alone.

He lifted his hat right off his head while people cheered, and made his way purposefully over to Tina. Applause merged into clapping for the next artiste, a grey-haired woman called Val wearing jeans and a gun holster. The evening carried on as before, until he took her home in the pick-up truck.

'Thank you for a lovely evening,' she said, staying her hand on the inside door handle of the truck.

'Thank *you*.' The engine puttered over at the gate. 'I want you to know . . . Well, I just want to say that . . . well . . . I admire you very much.'

'Me?' She watched him, transformed beside her. 'But I make such a *mess* of everything.'

'Well, I know you're going through a tough time and so forth, what with your mother-in-law, for example, and Rhona and . . . I know it can't be easy. And you've done an amazing job with that house, believe me you have.'

'Well—'

'I think you're very . . . very . . . I think you're very *competent*.'

She looked across at him and then at the windscreen. The tax disc was peeling off and the engine still stuttered. She felt a smile of pride come right up from her gut. 'Thank you.'

Moulin Rouge

A switch clicked on an electrical tub by the kettle, and a small red light went out. Tina removed the lid and stood back as steam poured out.

'You need something sterile to put it in,' she said, tapping at a jar in the tub which was too hot to hold. 'This is a bottle steamer, but it sterilises anything.'

Gabriel nodded. 'Show me how to work that thing. I'll do it every morning.'

She pulled out the empty make-up jar with the tips of her fingers and dropped it hurriedly on to the worktop.

'Eye gel?'

'It's sterile. Any jar will do, so long as you wash it first. Just put in this capful of water and switch it on here. The red light goes on. It takes about eight minutes, then it turns itself off.'

He took the jar and went to his room. Rhona came into the kitchen ready for town, and frowned. 'Where's he going?'

'Come on, you'll miss the bus.'

'I'm ready. Isn't he coming?'

'Oh yes,' said Tina wistfully. 'I hope so. Any minute now.'

Every morning for the next few days Gabriel delivered the jar to Tina's room, where she was waiting like an undercover agent at the door. When he had gone she lay on the bed with a syringe, drew out the contents of the jar, and gazed at a cobweb on the cornicing. Then she continued to lie in a state of deep relaxation for twenty minutes or so, her feet on the wall, humming 'The Teddy Bears' Picnic' to herself, or listening to the mobile as the penguins circled dizzily, fins out, beaks set in manic smiles: *How much is that doggie in the window?*

She rang Sarah Kelland to cancel the antenatal classes, saying things had not worked out as she'd planned, but she hoped to be going again next year. Sarah was sympathetic, but Tina replaced the receiver swelling with hope.

Tina was transformed during these days. She winked at Rhona, smiled at Bubbles, made cornflake cakes for Rhona's tuck box. She wore perfume and stockings, and breezed along the school pavements chirping 'Hello' at every Mrs Boreham-Green and pram-owner. Rhona cowered outside the school railings with Joel: 'Oh God. It's Mary Poppins!'

Gabriel, on the other hand, became more sluggish. He started like a man with a mission, all swanky and roguish, but then he began to get up later and later, handing the jar over with a yawn and heavy eyes. By Thursday, he did not emerge from his room at all, and Tina tapped until she heard a faint groan. She pushed the door ajar, and saw Gabriel wrapped in a twisted sheet, the heavy curtains still drawn.

'Gabriel?'

There was a grunt.

'Wakey, wakey!'

'What?'

'It's *Thursday*!'

'Yeah?'

'Yes. Thursday. Have you done it yet?'

There was a silence. 'Oh . . . Oh, God!' He rolled over.

'Gabriel, please. It's important.'

'Not today. I need a lie in.'

'But I'm *mid-cycle*!'

He groaned. 'Well, finish cycling, then.'

'Please, I'm *ovulating*!'

'Can't you do it somewhere else?'

'I need it *now*. My egg can't wait!' She walked over to him, tugged his arm, and heaved him protesting to the edge of the bed.

He lifted a pallid face and looked through slit eyes at her. 'I need a break, man.'

She marched to the door and then back again, and began to

untie her dressing gown slowly. She turned her back to him and flipped one shoulder off, and then the other. She let the pink gown slither to the floor and stood naked before him. Turning round, she saw that his face was still buried in the pillow.

There was an almighty thud as she pulled him once more and he fell off the bed, dragging her with him. He lay like a dead weight on top of her, and she raised her head from under his armpit. 'Gabriel – do it *now*!'

A thin shriek coincided with the door banging open.

'God! You two are *disgusting*!' squealed Rhona, and stamped down the stairs.

At around five o'clock the same day a couple turned up at the door. Tina looked at a short man with a velvet fez, a green kaftan and trousers that might once have been patchwork, but which now seemed a homogeneous mud colour. The woman was taller than him and wore some large black get-up with batwing sleeves. She turned a mottled, unsunned face to Tina and said, 'We've come for Bubbles.'

For a moment Tina thought that at last Bubbles was to be taken away, but these two looked unlikely to be from social services.

Surely not.

'Oh?'

'We were told it was here.'

'Yes?'

'We've come for healing.'

They were followed at seven o'clock by a pregnant Buddhist with swollen ankles and an aged biker with athlete's foot and a moon in Pisces. Beanie had spread the word. By the end of the week, hippies and assorted gentle zither-playing folk turned up to see Bubbles in droves, with psoriasis, piles and a need for harmony. Rhona or Gabriel showed them through to the annexe, where Bubbles sat in a cloud of patchouli and sandalwood, at one with the universe.

Tina said to Gabriel, 'I'm not sure about all this,' and 'Shouldn't she have a licence, or something?' but Gabriel reassured her she was more happy and more radiant than he had ever seen her, and to let her be. From time to time she emerged from the annexe and rifled amongst some leaves or herbs in the garden. At other times she stood over a simmering, bitter-smelling pot in the kitchen and sang to herself. Her hair grew into two thick clumps on either side of her centre parting, and she wore flowing tie-dyed cotton and tinted her eyelashes. Various colours.

Rhona snubbed Gabriel after she had found him with her mother. He felt a gnawing guilt surface in his throat and begin to choke him. If only someone would blame him for his father's death, he might free himself of the noose which seemed round him again. But not once since his arrival had anyone said, 'It's your fault! If you hadn't turned up, he'd still be here, mixing his paint!' and here was Tina, robbed of a longed-for child, and Rhona, bereft of friends and clinging on to the wreckage of a dying family, certain no one loved her. He stood for a moment in her little shoes and surveyed the world as she saw it. Growing up knowing that her mother had died so soon after her birth – a mother, a great umbrella of protection against the world – seemed like desertion. Then to lose a brother, whose short life had beamed most affection away from her, and whose death took all of it. Only Cameron left, and his slipping away so carelessly was a cruel evasion. Everyone she loved left her and it followed, therefore, that she was unlovable. Friends didn't swarm around her to change this opinion of herself. She was utterly alone in the world, but for a brother too ashamed to reveal himself. As far as he knew, Rhona still thought he was Wig, and he had basked in the glow of stardom, enjoying the frisson he knew she felt whenever he was near.

But the previous Wednesday she had found out before he could tell her, on account of the nine o'clock news reporting Wig's discovery in a brothel in the south of France, when she knew pretty well that Gabe was up the Co-op with Bubbles. For a day or two she said nothing, afraid he might go – whoever he was – if his cover were blown. At least, if he was not Wig in hiding from the world at large, then he could come and pick her up from school and impress the lot of them. She ignored the rumours that she had heard about him and Tina; until she saw the pair of them grappling on the floor in Gabe's bedroom.

'It's all true, and you've made a fool of me!' she screamed when Gabriel found her lying in a roll of carpet in the hall.

'What's all true?'

'Go away! All that sperm donation – it was just a front!'

'What?'

'What they say – it's all true! You and Mum being toyboys!'

'Me being a toyboy?' Gabriel laughed. 'Who says that?'

'Stop shouting at me!'

He tried to stroke her hair down the tube of carpet, but she recoiled from him, and rejected his pleas for her to come out.

He stood for a while, looking at the carpet roll – which sniffed from time to time – trying to think.

In the morning Rhona came down sulkily to find Gabriel perched on the edge of the kitchen table dressed all neat and perky, smelling sweet, and as wide awake as she had ever seen him at that time of the morning. His raven hair had been newly washed, as had his black T-shirt and jeans. He wore a black suede jacket and long pointed shoes studded with fake diamonds. He was clearly set to go somewhere special, and he and Tina were debating whether he should take his guitar, or just the case.

'What do you think?' he asked. Rhona said nothing and looked away at a packet of Shredded Wheat.

'Will I do as your escort to school?'

Slowly, she let her face smile, and Gabriel felt something fit into place, and stay there.

It was the last day of the summer term. No one much noticed him drop her off – or so it seemed – although she hugged him extravagantly in front of the school gates, but when he came to pick her up, a little crowd of Rhona's school chums gathered at a distance and smirked. He gave Rhona a bear hug and kissed her on the cheek. 'Let's wait for Joel,' she said, enjoying the performance.

One of the girls came over and hovered in front of them. 'Have you finished your new album yet?'

Rhona trod on his bejewelled foot, hard.

'No,' he said. 'No, I haven't.'

'Are you really staying at Rhona's?' asked another, galloping over.

'Yeah.' He felt curiously nervous, surrounded by these delving upturned faces, but then remembered why he was doing it. 'Yeah. It's great! I love it – especially Rhona!'

Rhona simpered, and a trill went around the group, which had moved closer and grown to seven or eight. A hard-faced little girl who he could have sworn was wearing mascara said, 'Is it true you're Wig, then?'

'Ah!' He felt Rhona jerk his sleeve and was suddenly overwhelmed with a feeling he'd never experienced, which hit him in the stomach like a punch. He wasn't sure how she would react; he didn't know how he was going to do it. He looked at her white face nestled between his sleeve and her hedge of hair, glowing with a pleasure he had never witnessed before, and he said, 'No, I'm not Wig – he's on the out, anyway.' He felt Rhona shrink, and said, 'I'm Rhona's brother.'

'Her *brother*?'

'Wow!'

'Rhona, you never said!'

He scooped Rhona over his shoulder and swung her round. Joel came scampering over, the girls were picked up by parents one by one, and they began to walk home.

'What did you have to say that for?' asked Rhona when he put her down.

'I thought you deserved the truth.'

She stood still on the pavement. He and Joel turned round to wait for her. She breathed heavily and watched his eyes. Then she ran at his waist crying, and shouting: 'Don't lie to me any more!'

He put his hands around her face: 'I won't. Not any more.'

It took a long time to sink in, but when it did, she was glad. He was a lifeboat washed up from the wreckage, and she climbed into it and felt safe.

That evening Bubbles looked dreadful. The skin around her eyes was white and cracked.

'Are you OK?' asked Tina.

'Of course I am!' She dunked a tea bag into a mug. 'But I'll tell you what: I don't think much of that eye gel of yours. Damn waste of money if you ask me!'

Sunlight

That weekend Tina started on the interior painting, and she continued to paint and lay carpets for several weeks. Rhona borrowed paints, remixed them, and painted the inside walls of the doll's house. The whole house at number twenty-three seemed full of colour, or dreams of colours. Colour charts were pinned to pieces of wall in all the rooms, and there were rainbows of colour on every surface: charts of every shade of yellow, green, blue and pink; samples of material, plain and patterned; tiny squares of carpet and vinyl flooring.

Tina painted the living room in Sunlight and the dining room in Terracotta. The hallway was Pacific Blue and the kitchen Honeybee Yellow. She painted her own bedroom in Strawberry Fool and Rhona's room in Texas Rose. Gabriel's room was Forget-Me-Not and the boxroom was going to be Dream Peach (a new stock of which was due in at Did-It-Myself at any time). The basement was painted a deep Jade Green, the bathroom Baby Blue, and the banisters and skirtings were Vanilla. Outside, the front door became Sweetheart Red and the old plastic 23 was replaced in brass.

When she had decorated all but two rooms, she gathered the paint-spattered rags that cluttered the skirting boards and the sheets covering the furniture. She cleaned all the brushes, producing sinkfuls of milky water in greens, blues and pinks. She washed around all the taps and scrubbed every surface. Then she set to work on the carpets. There was Dove Grey or Teddy, since that was what Cameron had stockpiled in the hallway, and there was some vinyl flooring at rock bottom discount from Did-It-

Myself. There was little furniture to move, and what she couldn't shift herself she left in place, rolling the carpet under one end of the bed, for example, and then the other. She fixed double-sided carpet tape around the rooms and left a trimming allowance of one inch of carpet on each wall. Then, pushing the carpet into the gap between the floor and the skirting and holding the trimming knife at an angle, she cut off the surplus and pressed the carpet firmly into place.

As she decorated and snipped, she was conscious some days of a knocking sound somewhere in the house which she had heard many times before, and she wondered what new activity Bubbles had undertaken with her fleets of visitors. From time to time she saw people arrive at the annexe, and leave later with a look of serenity. They came singly or in pairs, wandering up the front path and looking bewildered, searching for signs of mysticism and healing, or whatever they had come for. At first they had been a ragged-looking bunch, but lately they ranged from timeless hippies to neat businessmen and women with toddlers coated in eczema.

One afternoon she was sitting in the spare room sewing curtains. She was surrounded by yards of billowing calico, attaching rufflette heading tape to the tops of the curtains and contemplating the colour she would paint this room. She had left it till last because of a heavy old mirror against the wall which she was unable to move on her own. Gabriel had refused to touch it because of a weak back which would stop him gardening if it went again. She heard the knocking sound once more, and assumed Gabriel was doing up Bubbles' annexe, since there were no visitors. She finished machining all round outside the cords and stood up, gathering the material around her in clouds of ivory. She climbed on a chair and pulled the curtains up towards her, holding them against the window to see how much hem she needed to take up. But then the knocking sound came again, followed this time by a drilling noise, and she could clearly see Gabriel through the window quietly edging the flower borders in the sunshine.

She opened the window: 'Gabriel?'

He looked up and smiled.

'Gabe, what's that noise? Is Bubbles all right?'

He put down his pole-handled lawn edging knife and walked towards the house. 'Come down!' he shouted.

He left her in the kitchen, brushing bits of cotton off her dress, while he went to check on Bubbles. Then he put his head around the kitchen door. 'Come take a look at this.'

She followed him down the hall towards the annexe. As he opened the door to Bubbles' living quarters, it struck her that she had barely been more than a few feet inside since Gabriel's arrival. He had taken care of everything, and she had left Bubbles to her own devices. She felt a sudden panic at the thought of finding extreme squalor behind the door.

Instead, she stepped on to new carpet – Dove Grey – and smelt walls of fresh Terracotta paint. Gabriel opened a second door – of stripped pine finished in Oak woodseal – to reveal a newly decorated room in cream and apricot. The skirting boards were of newly treated wood, and a matching dado rail ran around the spacious room. In one corner an upholstered couch in rust-coloured velvet was covered with cushions; across the floor were thick patterned rugs and more cushions; and lining two walls were new wooden shelves covered in crystals, leafy plants, candles and blue glass bottles. On a low table some potion in a metal tray was being warmed by a lighted candle and giving off a smell of sandalwood. Above the thin streamers of smoke, towering on a ladder, drill in hand, stood Bubbles, wisps of orange hair escaping from the red gypsy scarf protecting her head. She smiled at Tina in surprise. 'Like it?'

Tina turned a full circle. It was beautiful. 'You didn't do all this yourself, did you?'

'I tried to help her,' said Gabriel, 'but she wouldn't have any of it. This here is all her own work.'

He led her into the adjoining two rooms: a small bedroom in Wheatgerm and Thyme Green with newly attached cornicing and mock centre rose and, leading off it, an en suite bathroom in Gooseberry Fool with wooden shelving and an intricately carved wooden toilet seat.

'Did it *all* herself. She's quite a woman,' said Gabriel proudly, 'my gran.'

Tina scratched her head and raised her eyebrows, smiling. 'It's wonderful!'

Bubbles came down the ladder to view it from the same position herself, and seemed pleased. Tina was impressed. The room felt homey and warm and full of magic. 'But how . . .? This must've cost a bit,' she said.

'Not really. I've made a pretty penny this past month, though.'

'You haven't been charging people, have you?'

'Oh no! I never charge. They just donate what they want.' She started to point around the room at gifts: these crystals, those pots, that painting, the bedcover, the bath . . .

Tina went to put the kettle on, feeling baffled and uplifted. Rhona, playing in the corner of the kitchen, said, 'Can I have some carpet for the garage?'

'We haven't got a garage.'

'For the doll's house, silly. I want to make an annexe.'

Tina went over to the doll's house and bent down to examine its new decorations. Rhona had made little paintpots out of ointment tube tops for the man of the house: the little rainbow-clad doll with fluffy hair. She claimed the Rainbow Man had done it all himself, but Tina knew differently. She watched Rhona cutting out a square of grey carpet; it seemed everyone was putting their house in order.

Keith Pooley was happy. Tina had invited him round to move some furniture, and she had never asked him for help before. Now she wanted his muscles to work with hers, moving together, lifting things in tandem, face to face. He shaved, and dressed carefully in clean overalls from the airing cupboard. He ruffled his hair, tugged it down over his ears, and whistled 'People will say we're in love' as he glided to the front door.

He looked at the room she was intending to paint; it was going to be a room for herself – a sewing room perhaps; she hadn't decided. The walls were covered in an old flower print wallpaper and hemmed in by a wardrobe, a divan, a giant mirror and a heavy teak chest of drawers. She took out all the clothes from the wardrobe and laid them on the divan, still on their metal hangers. Then they took one side each and tried to find a purchase.

'We'll lock these doors, I think,' said Keith. 'Else they'll pinch your fingers if they swing open.' He got back in position and counted to three. They lifted together and their faces stiffened. He watched the muscles flex along her upper arm and her jaw jut out as she held her breath. It was a hefty piece of furniture and took several lifts to move it a few feet from the wall.

'Hang! I dunno how they ever got him up here!' he said, wiping his forehead, and Tina left him to go and make a pot of tea. While she was gone, he inspected the chest. It was four feet tall and made of solid, dark wood. He began to take the drawers out carefully, to make it lighter to move. In the top twin drawers were photographs and letters on one side, and cheap bangles and headscarves on the other. He set them down gently in the middle of the room, casting his eyes away respectfully from their contents. In the next drawer were blouses and belts, and in the next, piles of folded dress fabric in different colours and prints. They were wide and heavy, but he managed them with a straight back. He started on the bottom two drawers, which were more difficult on account of their position. He squatted down, and had the penultimate drawer halfway across the room when he hesitated. He set it down carefully on top of the others and bent over it. There on the top was a sleepsuit, barely bigger than his outstretched hand. He picked it up by the arm, and the little all-in-one legs dangled down, just longer than his fingers. He looked at the label: 'New Born', and at the pile of similar suits underneath, all in shades of blue or cream. Next to them was a nest of socks, with feet shorter than his thumb. He held up a tiny pair, a plastic wire still attaching them to a price-tag. He put his hand into the drawer and pulled out a sunhat that might nicely fit a cricket ball. In the corner was a pile of bibs, the top one stained. He lifted it to his nose: it smelt sour and musty. He went back to the chest, pulled out the bottom drawer and peered into it. Neat piles of miniature cardigans and unworn vests in size 0–3 months filled one half. In the other side were brand new gadgets still in their boxes: a baby transmitter, a front carrier, a set of pacifiers, nappy cream and nipple pads. Next to them – tucked in the front – were a pair of red wellington boots and a home-made, unfinished pair of red dungarees. He lifted them out and hung them on his fingers. He gazed at them for a while, unsure whether the blur he saw was on account of losing focus or a tear he felt warming his cheek. Then he rose quietly to his feet and replaced the bottom two drawers reverently. He lifted the next drawer back into place to conceal them, and when Tina returned with the tea he was leaning against the chest.

'Took out a few drawers to make it lighter,' he said. 'No sugar for me, ta.'

After they had shifted the chest, there was only the mirror to move. It stood five feet high with a heavy gilt frame. The mirror itself was speckled and old, and Tina said it had been there when they moved in. There was a chain on the back, and they wrapped scarves around it to make a lever each side. They stood facing each other and heaved. He watched the strain on her face and, for an instant, he saw her pushing for a baby. He lurched too suddenly and the chain on his side broke. They were forced to push the mirror laboriously across the wall, eventually succeeding in turning it at a sufficient angle to steer it to the centre of the room and lean it against the chest.

Tina breathed with relief and went to pour him another cup of tea, but he was on his knees examining the skirting board. 'Well, blow me down!' he said, prodding at the skirting. 'You got a gap here – you've got two!' He scratched at the wallpaper and tore off a sleeve-shaped patch. 'You got a door here!'

Tina went over and scraped at the wallpaper too. She took a pen from her pocket and dug into the paper; it sheared crisply to reveal the jambs and hinges of a door. He went to fetch some tools, and returned with a screwdriver. There was no doorhandle, so he pushed the screwdriver into the keyhole, trying to pull the catch across.

Suddenly the door fell open, and swung into a small room. They both stood in the doorway and caught their breath. It was dimly lit by a casement window covered in ivy. And as they opened the rusty catch and pulled the ivy away, tearing at its clinging tendrils in excitement, the sun poured in on the yellowed walls and flooded them with sunlight.

He watched her standing still at last, hot and radiant, a pile of ivy at her feet like wrapping paper, the early evening sun gilding her hair into a halo. They both breathed heavily and their pulses pounded. In his heart he told her that he loved her. What he actually said was, 'Crikey!' Then he added, 'A window!'

Fiesta Flame

It was a hot Tuesday in August; school had broken up some two weeks before, and there was a stillness around the playgrounds and pavements. Tina skirted the shelves in the newsagent's next to the Co-op for reading material that might arouse Gabriel's interest. All the magazines in question were on the top shelf, out of her reach. She asked a tall man who was examining one if he could pass her the one next to it, picturing a scantily clad woman on all fours looking round. He obliged nervously, and she leafed through it with disappointment. All the poses were the same. She asked the tall man if he might just pass her the next one, featuring a scantily clad woman on all fours with stilettos. He handed it to her and scratched his nose, as though disclaiming her. Tina leafed through this one and found that the models were no different, except there was one called Tina who sat on some white steps in a Greek village wearing broderie anglaise and no knickers. 'Slut!' muttered Tina, and then tugging the man on the sleeve: 'Is that all there is?'

He seemed to sink into his collar, and handed her another three, whispering, 'That's it now – that's the lot.'

Tina didn't dare ask him to replace any. She took all five to the cash desk and screwed her face in horror at the prices.

'Oh, isn't it Mrs Morrison?' came a voice behind her in the queue. 'I hardly recognised you without your overalls!'

It was the head, Mrs Stacey, whose own head seemed stuck on the top of her blue dress like a child's drawing. Next to her was that councillor woman, who nodded hello.

'Oh, do you two know each other?' asked Mrs Stacey, rotating.

Tina waited while Mrs Boreham-Green or Boring-White digested the front covers of her magazines, and said, 'Yes!' Then she bundled them up, hugged them to her chest – bottoms outward – and said, 'Just getting a bit of holiday reading for Rhona!'

Outside the newsagent's she bit her lip. Then she smiled, finished her shopping, and went to find Gabriel.

As she approached the front gate she heard music coming from the garden. She rounded the hedge and saw Bubbles, Gabriel and assorted strangers holding hands in a circle and moving in unison to some eastern-sounding music. At the same time she noticed a figure standing watching it, not far from the gate: it was Mrs Stacey.

'I don't think Rhona is in,' said Tina, defensively.

'It's not Rhona I've come to see,' said Mrs Stacey, turning stiffly.

Tina felt leaden. She wasn't in the mood for more chastisement, however gentle. She didn't want to hear how Rhona wasn't coping or how *she* wasn't coping or how she could improve everything with psychologists and therapists or more time together punching cushions or discussing death. 'I'm a bit busy, just now.'

'It's not you I've come to see! It's Bubbles! I've got an appointment at four o'clock for my neck and frozen shoulder. She's done wonders for Felicity!'

'Oh,' said Tina. 'Well . . . would you like some tea or something, while you're waiting?'

'Oh, I'm fine. I do love this circle dancing, don't you? I'm going to ask about it when they've finished. Felicity swears by it.' She nodded over to the circle where Tina now saw the councillor gliding around between a pregnant kaftan and Beanie. 'Do you think she'd be interested in helping at the summer fête?'

The music stopped, and Gabriel beckoned Mrs Stacey to go and join them. Then the cassette recorder started up again, Beanie sat cross-legged tapping a pair of hand drums, and Gabriel taught everyone the steps to a Red Indian dance he'd learnt from Keith Pooley. Tina rubbed her eyes, and went to turn the kettle on.

The summer fête was that weekend – the first in August – and took place in the school playing field. There was a coconut shy, Bowling-for-the-Pig, Pin-the-tail-on-the-Donkey, and Guess-the-weight-of-the-Cake. In one corner there were donkey rides provided by an old donkey called Deirdre, and in another a small band had set up its electronic equipment with giant speakers and a spaghetti of black wires. Down one side of the field was a tea tent covered in bunting, outside which a clown was selling raffle tickets for a giant bear wrapped in polythene. On the other side of the field stretched stalls of every description, with a long tail of people queueing in front of one in particular.

Rhona approached it and saw 'FORTUNES TOLD with Bubbles' Ball of Crystal'. Bubbles was hidden from view behind a screen, and Gabriel was taking money, leaping around from person to person like someone possessed. Rhona went to the head of the queue and lurked around Gabriel, basking in his presence and the awe she might inspire in school chums who happened to pass by. This was her brother, and she wanted everyone to know it.

Then Tina arrived and he asked Rhona to take over, while he walked off in the direction of the tea tent. She stood staring at the two of them, forgetting to give change to a bald man with twins: they were walking far too close together for her liking.

She saw Kelly Porter in the queue with her mother, and smiled. Kelly looked away, possibly out of embarrassment at her mother, who was telling a friend, 'We really only came for the bookstalls – Kelly can't get enough of them!'

'Nor Flavia!' said her friend. 'She'd practically devoured the works of Dickens by the time she was ten.' Rhona pictured Flavia munching her way through a fat volume of *Oliver Twist*, and frowned.

Joel saw her as he walked past with a toffee apple. 'Hey, Rhona!' he called. 'I found out what was in it!'

'In what?'

'The chocolate cake.'

'What, then?'

He waited until she had finished giving change and had turned away from the stall. 'Well, it's not very nice.'

'Well *what*?'

'Promise you won't get upset?'

'Why should I? I'm better now. What was it?'

'Shit!' he whispered.

'What's the matter?'

'No. Shit. It was shit.'

'What?'

'It was. Beanie said. Best shit he'd ever had.'

She saw he was serious, and her face collapsed. 'You mean I've eaten someone's poo?'

'I knew you'd get upset!'

She ran around the field shrieking, leaving the fortune teller's stall to fend for itself. She'd eaten some old hippy's poo and Joel had told her. She could never speak to him again. Joel nibbled his nails, and thought he had better go and watch the band.

At four o'clock Rhona was walking from stall to stall searching for Gabriel. She could see Tina was at the fortune teller's stand, but he wasn't with her. He wasn't in the tea tent either. She could hear music coming over the speakers, and in the distance she could see Keith Pooley standing on the low stage with the band; the music had become just guitars and drums for this number. As she moved closer she noticed girls from her class at school dancing in unison in front of the stage. She quickened her step and the music stopped. 'OK, that was a Red Indian dance,' she heard Gabriel say, and the music started again, only this time Keith was crooning a country and western number. There was Hayley Farrow stepping it out to the music, and behind her Kelly Porter and a bunch of other boys and girls from year six; they were watching Joel and Gabriel who stood in front moving gracefully over the grass. Gabriel had his back to them all, demonstrating the steps: 'Right, two, three, four – Left, two, three, four – Split those heels! *And* . . . grapevine right!' Rhona gaped. Some of the children were moving clumsily, but Joel had it to a T, doing quarter-turns in unison with Gabriel and stomping in perfect time to the music. Children seemed to come from nowhere, and even as she looked the group grew to a crowd and started spilling over to the edges of the equipment van and around the coconut shy, and Deirdre the donkey was halted in her stride as a 'half-turn, shuffle, and grapevine left' had her boxed in by a group of children. Rhona rushed forward towards Gabriel and tugged at his sleeve, confused and somehow hurt.

He yelped with glee and grabbed hold of her arms, making the movements for her. Within a minute she was stepping it out with the rest of them – and they could all see her: with Gabriel.

A few specks of rain hit the stage, and when the tune ended the band members looked at the sky and muttered. Hayley Farrow came over to Rhona and said, 'Your brother's so *cool*!' and then she asked if Rhona wanted to come to tea sometime. The rain was falling in fat heavy drops and people were running for cover.

'Yes,' Rhona nodded vigorously. 'That would be nice!' As soon as she'd said it, she wished she had sounded less available, but she felt elated, letting the rain ruin her hair and turn it into an even more unruly frizz. By now people were crowding for shelter in the tea tent and Gabriel, Keith and Joel were struggling to cover the electrical equipment with a huge tarpaulin, while the other members of the band were moving what they could into a van.

'Get in the van!' Gabriel shouted over to her. 'You'll catch your death!

The sky had turned to blue-black and was giving off a dull greenish light. There was a bright flash of lightning followed by a rumble of thunder. Keith Pooley came over and took hold of her where she stood. 'Come on into the van.' He wiped clutter off the front seat with his hand and helped her in.

'Guess what!' she said. 'I'm making new friends!'

'That's wonderful!' Then, turning to go, he poked his head back into the van. 'But don't you forget who your most loyal friends are.' He nodded towards Joel who was drenched and trying to help Beanie carry a speaker. 'You get in the van too!' shouted Keith, and Joel, protesting, went to join Rhona.

They said nothing, watching the rain on the windscreen and listening to the roaring thunder.

'Want a liquorice shoelace?' he asked at last, holding out a crumpled paper bag.

'What's in it?'

He sighed, and his face turned white with a crack of lightning. 'Just liquorice.'

'OK then.'

It was still raining heavily a quarter of an hour later, and Keith went to fetch Bubbles and Tina to offer them a lift home in the equipment van.

'It's only round the corner!' said Tina. 'We can walk!'

There was another clap of thunder. 'You'll get drenched in this. Come on, I'm giving the others a lift anyway!'

Bubbles sat in the front, sandwiched between Keith and Tina, and Gabriel sat in the back with Rhona and Joel, amidst speakers and microphones. He picked up a guitar and started plucking. 'How long you been playing?' he asked Keith, leaning close to the back of Tina's neck.

'Oh . . . years now – fifteen, maybe. You play?'

'No. Not my instrument.'

It sounded odd to Rhona, watching the long fumbling fingers which until recently she had thought could dance over the strings with his eyes closed. Perhaps he could play other instruments – she hadn't thought to ask – but she was too busy watching him leaning on the back of Tina's seat to think about that right now.

The windscreen-wipers became inadequate as the rain washed down the glass more thickly than ever, and the light seemed to have gone out of the day. Bubbles started to sing:

> 'Dark is the evening, silent the hour,
> Oh who is the minstrel by yonder high bower?
> Who sings Lady, love, will you come with me now
> Come and live merrily underneath the bough,
> I'll pillow thy head where light fairies tread
> If thou wilt but wed with young Ned of the Hill . . .'

'Can Keith come for tea?' asked Rhona.

'Oh, well . . .' said Tina, wondering what they had in to eat and feeling agitated, 'of course. Drop us off and stay for tea.'

'That's very kind of you,' said Keith, 'but I promised I'd get this van back by five. It's my neighbour's, and he's got a gig in Dorset this evening. I'd ask you to my place, only . . .' Hang! If he'd only thought, there were so many little things he would want to do in preparation for a visit from Tina. He would provide a fresh hand towel in the downstairs cloakroom and some lavender soap; he would buy a whole range of cakes from Trinder's Bakery; he'd buy pink roses and carnations and arrange them in vases in every room; he'd tidy up his workshop so's he could show it to Rhona; he'd put that lace tablecloth on . . . ' . . . only the place is a bit of a tip.'

'*We* don't mind!' said Rhona, 'Look at *our* place! You can't get much more of a tip than that!'

'Well, I've no cake – hang! I don't think I've even got any biscuits in!'

'I'm not that into cake at the moment,' Rhona shot a glance at Joel, 'speaking for myself. Oh *please*, Keith! I've never seen your house!'

He looked at Tina for help. He didn't want to reject an opportunity. 'Well, why not? It's nothing special, mind.'

'We really don't mind at all,' said Tina. 'We can just wait there till the rain stops, if you like.'

> 'Young Ned of the Hill has no castle nor hall,
> No bowmen nor spearmen to hurry at his call,
> But one little archer, all blessed with great skill,
> Has shot a bright dart for young Ned of the Hill . . .'

The last days in August were windy, and the trees rustled like a tide coming in. Tina was in the bathroom, looking at a window. She knew she should go away and come back in ten minutes, but she just sat there, staring. Above it was another window with a blue line running across it, and she watched, as the damp seeped up through the bottom window, for signs of blue. Surely that was a smudge of blue at the side? Or was it the light? She blinked, and looked about her. Maybe if she thought of something else for a while she would see more clearly when she looked back. She rested her eyes on the cold tap. Nothing interesting there. She glanced at the bottles of talcum powder, skin lotions, ointments and shampoo on the window sill, and at a pink bath towel of Rhona's left in a pool on the floor. The blue bath mat was threadbare and needed a wash. The white marbled vinyl overlapped at the bath and needed trimming a quarter of an inch. She sat on the closed toilet seat and shut her eyes. Ten, nine, eight . . . She opened them. Was that a faint blue line? It was hard to tell. Could she be a very *little* bit pregnant?

She ran into the kitchen where Gabriel was attaching a garden hose to the tap. He said it was a line and it was blue. He picked her up and hugged her. He sat her down and made her tea. He raised his arms in the air and did a little dance: 'Yes!' he kept saying, 'Yes!'; and outside in the garden the hose wriggled and sprayed the garden shed.

Tina gazed out of the window, smiling, and watched some house sparrows chirping in the cherry tree, sharing a feeling with them, at last.

'Just promise me one thing,' said Gabriel. 'Just promise me – you can have tea, can't you? – just promise me I can be your birthing partner. Right! We'll do yoga – can you do yoga? – and we'll have organic veggies. No red meat, you hear? And folic acid – are you taking it? And we'll have to fix a room up. And we'll go out shopping for baby clothes – there's loads to get!'

There was a lot to be done. She would have to take all the baby clothes out of the drawer, she thought, and hang them up.

The months passed, and Tina grew bigger and rosier and more and more happy. She decorated the boxroom at last in Dream Peach and added rainbows, hung mobiles, cleaned cupboards and hemmed new curtains with bears on them. Keith made her a new crib with carved bears at the head, and she asked him to take the old cot away from the attic. She and Rhona made patchwork cot bumpers, towel bibs, fleece jackets and soft toys. They spent whole afternoons in Mothercare, making lists, playing the musical mobiles and trying on nighties. Rhona designed a Baby Alarm, which was an elaborate system of cords the baby could pull if it woke up and felt like milk (white cord), nappy change (blue cord), or cuddle (red cord). They went for long walks and looked at sheep. Tina found herself welling with tears at soap operas, birds and grazing cows.

The swell of the summer produced fruits on the trees, lush grass, nettles and posses of ducklings; autumn galloped into a cold winter with coats that would no longer button up; then crocuses peeped up through the soil by the church and fat sheep smiled at her knowingly: she was part of it all. She had been away and come home. In the field next to the church she lay on the kind warm earth and smiled and grew.

Dream Peach

Early in May Tina felt a spasm of pain in her side while she was clearing the hall. She stood for a moment against the wall, surveyed the debris that had blocked the door for months, and continued her work. There were half-full tins of paint, paintbrushes suspended on nails in jars of solvent, rags with multicoloured smudges, scissors, chisels and bits of skirting board. She collected them into boxes which she pushed against the walls, and then swept the floor. She leant on the broom as another pain seared her belly, and she closed her eyes and smiled.

Bubbles made her a raspberry leaf tea and they both sat in the kitchen, watching for movement under Tina's flowered smock. A limb moved across her abdomen like a kitten under a bedcover. It moved more slowly than usual, and Bubbles laid her hands on Tina's belly, saying: 'It'll come the day after tomorrow.'

In the evening Gabriel and Rhona rubbed her skin with lavender oil. She knew her time had come, but she said nothing. The hallway was clear and she felt there was a way for the baby to come now. All night she lay watchful, welcoming each pain like a long-expected guest.

The milk float came and went. At four thirty she bathed, and again at six. At eight thirty she saw them all off – Rhona to school and Gabriel and Bubbles to town – waving, doe-eyed and saying nothing.

At midday the pains were ten minutes apart. She made a phone call and then went to the hearth rug, sat on the floor, and pulled the soles of her feet together, humming deeply.

After a few hours the contractions were only a minute apart

and she was unable to remember anything Sarah Kelland had told her. She began to rock and crawl into new positions. She felt busy and excited, took in deep breaths, and on each out breath let out a long, low 'Maaaah!' She could see the chimney breast with its dark opening into the room, and she chanted louder and longer and felt removed from everything except the child fighting to come out of her.

She was aware of being led into a car, clinging on to a sleeve, eyes closed, concentrating. She opened them to a low-lit room and a uniformed girl who was attaching two thick elastic straps around her lower and upper abdomen. 'We'll just pop you on the monitor for twenty minutes.'

Tina was sitting up, unable to move. Although she tried not to look at it, she could see the trace on the monitor showing her contractions, and because it could detect their strength before she felt them, fear tightened the pain. Twenty minutes passed slowly, then forty. She asked if the baby was in distress. It wasn't. It was just procedure because the trace wasn't 'picture book'. The midwife was called Kim and kept up an irritating babble of small talk. Tina wanted to lie down. Every time she had a contraction her bottom rose off the chair like a cartoon character sitting on tintacks. She couldn't imagine a more uncomfortable position to be in for heavy contractions.

An hour later she was still strapped to the monitor, wriggling, hearing how Kim's sister-in-law had bought shoes for two right feet. She eventually got down on her knees, pulling the contraption with her, and began to chant again and feel in control of the pain. The midwife detached the straps before they tore the wires from the monitor, and disappeared to fill the birthing pool. After twenty minutes she returned and said that if Tina wanted the pool she would just have to be 'popped back on the monitor' for twenty minutes. After twenty minutes, though, the trace wasn't 'picture book' so she had to stay on it longer. Tina was becoming distraught. The contractions were relentless and she could see from the monitor they were the strongest yet.

She was given an internal examination. Kim didn't seem to register her contraction and the pain was overwhelming. 'Hours to go yet. That's a nice ring – is it a diamond?' She was six centimetres dilated. It was nearly midnight.

She liked being in the pool, and floated in and out of pain. But to her horror, Kim had procured an underwater monitor, and began prodding her tender belly in the pool. Tina felt trapped. She couldn't manoeuvre her body into a comfortable position, and lay crumpled like a deflating lilo, her back aching, as Kim said, 'I hear you're a bit of a DIY expert. Been doing up a room for the baby? My hubby's into that. Can't stop him once he gets going – which is every weekend! Once he decided to enlarge our living room and he knocked down a load-bearing wall! I'm afraid we'll just have to pop you back on the monitor.'

She asked what was wrong, and a wave of pain swept over her, stronger than ever. She let out a colossal bray, and kept it long and low and controlled. She wanted to be left in peace to deal with the pain. She would block out everything. She would block out this woman with her brittle chit-chat and focus on letting go.

'Oh, nothing wrong! Just not ideal! Are you naturally curly? Mmmm? Ooooh, I'd love hair like that!'

It was two in the morning. She was back on the monitor in too much pain to complain and, she dimly thought, probably not the sort of person who could. She had been in hospital for six hours, and in a comfortable position for only twenty minutes. The pain was relentless now. Breath was grabbed, caught, held, and then wailed out in grunts that turned to screams; more breath, pounding in the head, leaving the body, leaving the place behind, more screams, controlled to braying, breathing, breathing, return to earth (' . . . and anyway, my sister reckons if you perm your hair too often . . .'), and prepare again for pain, already building, building . . . 'If I could only—' but it was too late. Breath torn from the air in gulps and given out on the crest of pain – but no, worse to come, and worse, and worse – then slowly retreating. 'If I could—' and again, and again. Relentlessly.

At four in the morning the midwife said she would have to break the waters. Tina signalled a no and was aware of a babble of disapproval. 'I'm afraid the birth's progressing too slowly, Christina. It's nothing to worry about, it'll just speed things up.

You see, at the moment it's going too slowly.'

'Too slowly for whom?' she said inside her head. *Leave me alone.*

More babble. More pain. Wave upon wave. No time to explain. She wanted to say it wasn't fair. It wasn't fair to argue with someone who couldn't argue back. She didn't want any interference. She was afraid the cord might drop round the baby's neck if the waters were broken. She felt the baby pushing inside her: it was working hard, she was working hard. There was no problem. She wanted to wander off into some undergrowth like a squaw and lay this baby into the world in a quiet, secret space. She wanted to give birth and the midwife was twiddling with machinery and behaving as if this were an operation, some sort of hospital manoeuvre that produced a baby – nothing to do with her. She was too exhausted to resist. She howled as the crochet hook went in; it felt very intrusive and wrong. And then she had to 'pop back on the monitor' for another twenty minutes to see what effect it had all had.

Tina bellowed the most disconcertingly loud notes she could to make it clear she was distressed. She did this very deliberately because she could no longer talk: words seemed to have left her. She wanted to strangle Kim with the monitor strap, but felt trapped by some strange vulnerable courtesy that had hounded her all her life. The midwife kept wittering on about ideal traces and clothes from high street stores. 'Oooh! That's a lovely nightie. Did you get that from Marks?'

Tina tried to speak: 'B . . . B . . .' and was scooped up by the pain. She shook her head. She needed silence, total peace to concentrate on the contractions. The baby needed her full attention. It was a monumental struggle for the tiny creature: it didn't want to hear about nighties. Pain flooded in; she rose off the chair, the thick straps held her down, pulling her searing belly. 'B . . . B . . .' she tried again, and failed. She took a great gulp of air: 'B . . . British Home Stores!'

This seemed to delight Kim, who rattled on about good value and underwear.

Tina had disappointed herself. With the next contraction she rose off the chair, bellowed an almighty Moo, and ripped the straps off her, flinging herself on to the bed and screaming, begging for some respite.

She trembled and vomited and was aware of Kim talking about 'transition' and 'tea break' and then seeming to evaporate.

Tina started to take control of the birth. She knelt on the floor over a chair, and for the first time since she'd come into hospital she felt relaxed. She wanted to push. A temporary midwife who materialised form behind her said she wasn't sure if she was dilated enough. She examined Tina's notes and supposed it was all right. But Tina knew it was right. She pushed with each contraction and felt controlled and powerful. She galloped across plains. She flew from clifftops. She soared. She pushed. Kim reappeared and said it would be another hour at least. Then she said the cord was round the baby's neck and she would have to just ask Tina to pop back on the monitor.

But Tina was unstoppable. She was in a position she'd practised. She knew the baby was coming and was determined not to go near the monitor or sit on a chair or reply to the outside world. She felt gravity on her side, and remembered Sarah Kelland saying it was important to 'let go', emotionally as well as physically.

She was aware of someone else now, stroking her arm, barely touching her: a presence. She held her pelvis wide and let the earth pull her into itself. She saw Cameron mixing paint and she let him float away, peacefully. The past welled up as a pool of magenta light, and she replaced it with a warm peach that flooded the room. Now the pushing was burning, red hot, and she felt she would rip open. With the next contraction she left everything behind. She stopped worrying about tearing and let go completely: the baby's head came out, and she was delivered.

She was passed back between Tina's legs, with Kim saying My God, it shouldn't have happened for at least another hour, heavens above. The tiny being gazed at Tina with wide open blue eyes: an avid, searching look. Tina knelt on the floor, trembling, holding her, speechless. She sat back in a pool of blood, hugging her ('. . . can you just shift your bum? It's getting all over the floor . . .').

The cord was a beautiful translucent blue, wound like a perfect rope, and shorter than she'd remembered. She held the little girl up and shared the slate blue eyes full of wonderment. The room was filled with a magnificent bleachy smell, rich and earthy. It covered the baby's head and stayed with her, so that Tina could find her for the next few days as a sheep would find its lamb. It was the most heavenly smell she had ever known.

The sun was coming up, and filled the room with warm bands of peach and gold.

She sat in a seat-shaped bath and watched the water turn blood red as a nurse supervised her washing; she was stitched by two venomous women with rubber gloves and dripping colds, an agony which did not serve the baby and therefore felt like agony; she was moved, hobbling, to a ward and offered a soggy piece of toast which tasted like a feast; and all the while yearning to hold the baby in her arms again. It was wheeled to her bedside in a plastic trolley and she lifted it out; she smelt it was hers.

The heavens opened. Never, not even with the first baby, had she felt such elation. All around the tiny head was a cloud of love. Her little eyes gazed wide and guileless into Tina's; her cheeks glowed, her damp head nuzzled. She was radiant. The warm plasticine fingers gripped hers, damp and firm, with long spatulate tips that wouldn't let go. Tina laid her on the bed next to her face and they studied each other for hours: damp-eyed gazing from the mother and long, frank, artless looks from the baby. Her eyes were still wet with joy when Gabriel arrived.

'Why didn't you *tell* me? Oh, just look at her! I came last night and they wouldn't let me in. Oh, can I hold her? Look at her! Why didn't you *say*?'

'I don't know.' Tina held the baby out towards Gabriel's arms. 'Perhaps I wanted to do it myself.'

'This is taking DIY too far! Oh, look at those little hands! She's got my nose!'

'I don't think so.'

He leant over the baby, pushing his hair back behind his ear, jittery with excitement. He took off his dark jacket and prepared to hold her, his smiling anticipation seeming to transform him into a child. 'What's her name?'

'Angela.'

'Angela! That suits her. Not Gabriella, then?' But Gabriel was inspecting the little wrist tag. 'What's this? Angela *Pooley*? Why've they put *his* name down, for God's sake?'

'Because,' said Keith, emerging from the corridor with a flask of cocoa and looking tired and puffy, 'that's her name.'

Tina gave Gabriel a sheepish look, then laughed. 'I decided against DIY in the end. She's a little Pooley, and I love her!'

Gabriel's mouth was still open. He looked from Tina to Keith, and back again. Now he came to think of it, they had been spending a lot of time together lately. Then he looked at the baby. 'You mean . . . she's not . . . mine?'

'Nope.'

'You mean, this little bundle of gorgeousness, this little scrumptious cuddlekins, has absolutely nothing to do with me whatsoever?'

Tina shook her head.

Gabriel sighed and held the baby closer.

'I'm not sure I'd say that,' said Keith, sitting on the bed. 'If you hadn't turned up at my door, she mightn't be here now.'

Slowly, Gabriel looked up and smiled. 'Well,' he sighed at last, 'congratulations! She *is* lovely.'

Night fell, and the patch of sky through the ward window changed from white through blue to black. Tina hadn't slept for two days, and she couldn't sleep now. She studied the closed eyelids of her baby, delicately veined in a lace of dark grey and magenta. She remembered the absolute peace that only came from being slept on by a baby. It was the early hours before she drifted into a deep, happy sleep, the baby nestled in her armpit. At four o'clock a midwife woke her to check that she was sleeping and to inspect her nipples. Tina smiled: everything was OK. Everything. She didn't feel passive or pushed around. They served her: all she had to do was press the buzzer for one of these women to come running to her side. She was a mother. A proud, elated, exhausted mother. She felt like every contented sheep or cow lying fatly by its young, as she took in deep breaths of the satin hair and watched the baby diligently watching her.

* * *

In the morning Keith returned with Rhona, and Gabriel brought Bubbles who carried an enormous picnic hamper of ham sandwiches, and sang:

> ' . . . How gloriously the sun does shine!
> How pleasant is the air!
> I'd rather rest on my true love's breast
> Than any other where . . .'

They were joined later by Mrs Ferabee who brought Joel, three babygrows wrapped in crêpe paper, and a Kodak flash camera.

Tina and Keith held the baby on the bed, snuggling closely; Gabriel put his arm around Bubbles and squeezed in on the left of the bed; Joel put his arm round Rhona and squeezed her on the right. Rhona squeezed him back. Mrs Ferabee motioned them all to move a bit closer into the frame, and took the picture which would decorate the hallway of 23 Church Road for generations to come.

The camera clicked and flashed at their happy faces and, for that moment at least, as they smiled into the future, everyone was exactly where they wanted to be.